THIS IS NOT A STORY

Denis Diderot

THIS IS NOT A STORY

and Other Stories

Translated with
an Introduction by
P. N. Furbank

University of Missouri Press
Columbia and London

University of Missouri Press, Columbia, Missouri 65201
Printed and bound in the United States of America

5 4 3 2 95 94 93 92

Library of Congress Cataloging-in-Publication Data

Diderot, Denis, 1713–1784.
[Short stories. English]
This not a story and other stories / Denis Diderot ; translated with an introduction by P. N. Furbank.
p. cm.
Stories translated from the French.
Includes bibliographical references.
ISBN 0-8262-0815-0 (alk. paper)
1. Diderot, Denis, 1713–1784—Translations into English.
I. Furbank, Philip Nicholas. II. Title.
PQ1979.A25 1991
843′.5—dc20 91-27703
CIP

∞™ This paper meets the requirements of the American National Standard for Permanence of Paper for Printed Library Materials, Z39.48, 1984.

Designer: Elizabeth K. Fett
Typesetter: Connell-Zeko Type & Graphics
Printer and binder: Thomson-Shore, Inc.
Typeface: Bodoni

CONTENTS

NOTE ON THE TEXT AND TRANSLATION

Diderot's stories present enormously complicated textual problems, since the manuscript copies display all degrees of accuracy or carelessness, and Diderot continued to tinker with his texts and make interpolations until the end of his life; moreover, new manuscripts have continued to turn up even in quite recent years. I have consulted the texts provided by Jacques Proust in *Diderot, Quatre contes* (1964), by Herbert Dieckmann in *Diderot, Contes* (1963), and by Paul Vernière in his edition of Diderot's *Oeuvres philosophiques* (n.d.)

The question of the layout of dialogue is also extremely complicated, no two manuscripts or printed versions adopting exactly the same system, and almost all containing internal inconsistencies. It is an important matter, since Diderot was, plainly, deliberately experimenting in these matters and exploring different ways of superimposing one dialogue upon another. I have taken the liberty of making adjustments of my own here and there, in the cause of clarity or consistency.

In my translation I have tried, at the cost perhaps of oddity here and there, to stick rather closely to Diderot's sentence construction, considering it an essential element in his style. Two problems of vocabulary proved more or less insoluble. Diderot continually uses the epithet *honnête,* and, for curious and important reasons of social history, the term is not really translatable into English; thus I have had to render it, variously, as "decent," "gentlemanly," "honorable," "of good will," and so on. Secondly, the term *moeurs,* which figures prominently in "Supplement to Bougainville's *Voyage,*" means both "morals" and "customs," and I have had to render it by one or the other of these, according to the context, with some loss to Diderot's meaning. (The term *manners* would, once, have been an accurate translation, but, again no doubt for important historical reasons, it has hopelessly narrowed in its meaning.)

THIS IS NOT A STORY

INTRODUCTION

The world is not short of admirers of Diderot as a novelist, that is to say of the author of *Rameau's Nephew, The Nun,* and *Jacques the Fatalist.* It is curious, therefore, that his short stories—there are five of them, all in their way remarkable—have been left a little in the shade. It has not always been so. Balzac thought Diderot's "This Is Not a Story" "one of the grandest fragments of the history of the human heart"; he said that it "sweated truth in every sentence."[1] Again, Diderot's tale "The Two Friends from Bourbonne," with its impetuous abruptness of style and its romanticization of the outlaw, helped to set Schiller on a new path as a writer. Goethe, indeed, alluding to the same story, depicts Diderot as providing a program for young German writers in general: "His children of nature pleased us very much, his brave poachers and smugglers enchanted us."[2] It became the thing for Goethe's friends to praise Diderot at the expense of the "genteel" French tradition and to claim him for their own. "In everything for which the French blame him," writes Goethe in his *Autobiography,* "he is a true German."[3]

Already, in saying so much, we run up against a fact never far from our consciousness when thinking of Diderot: I mean the strangeness of his publishing history. For "The Two Friends from Bourbonne" and "Conversation of a Father with His Children" were known in Germany before they were in France, having first come out in a German translation by Salomon Gessner, in a volume containing Gessner's own *Idylls;* only in the following year, 1773, was Diderot's French text published. These stories thus anticipated the pattern of *Rameau's Nephew,* which first appeared in 1805, twenty years after Diderot's death, in a German translation by Goethe, and had its first appearance in French (in a garbled translation back from Goethe's German!) in 1821. As for his remaining three tales, they had to wait until fifteen years or so after Diderot's death to appear in printed form. During his lifetime these, like most of his truly original writings, came out merely in a manuscript journal, the *Correspondance littéraire,* run by his friend Melchior Grimm. The *Correspondance littéraire* was a sort of running report on French cultural affairs intended for the eyes of foreign princes. It never had more than fifteen or so subscribers, so that for a work to have appeared there cannot really be considered "publication."

Thus Diderot as a novelist was not writing for a public, and the reasons for this are complicated. He had good reason to be wary, for an early philosophical work, his freethinking *Letter on the Blind,* had earned him a spell in prison; but other and deeper reasons also seem to enter in. The truth is that, though an intensely sociable man and a figure very much in the public eye, he had none of that marvelous rapport with a public possessed by Voltaire and by Rousseau. He could be clumsy in his direct dealings with the public; and, more to the point, the whole notion of a "public" and public opinion baffled and disturbed him and, for that very reason, gripped his imagination. Thus it is no accident that this fiction writer without an audience (for his German audience was an accident) should have evolved a theory of fiction profoundly concerned with *audiences:* the audiences for our conduct and the audiences for our stories. Another consequence of not writing for publication was that Diderot was encouraged to work out his conception of fiction for himself and from first principles. Apart from an early work, *Indiscreet Jewels,* which was in the familiar genre of the French libertine novel, his work is very little influenced by French models.

His five stories were all written in the same fairly brief period, between 1770 and 1772 (he was then in his late fifties); and they represent a kind of experiment. The series began with "The Two Friends from Bourbonne," which, like some other of his writings, first arose from a hoax or "mystification," involving his friend Grimm. In the summer of 1770, Diderot, accompanied by Grimm, paid a visit to his birthplace, Langres, in Burgundy, and during it he spent a week or two in the nearby spa of Bourbonne-les-Bains, where two friends of theirs, Madame de Maux and her daughter Madame de Prunevaux, were taking the waters. The two women were bored and were amusing themselves by writing stories, and Diderot, upon joining them, proposed a conspiracy, by which he would pass off a story of his own as being by them. The plot involved a mutual friend of theirs, the young atheistical philosopher Jacques-André Naigeon. Naigeon had sent them a recently published story by the Marquis de Saint-Lambert, entitled "The Two Friends: A Tale of the Iroquois." Friendship indeed had been a fashionable topic that year. There had been a play by Beaumarchais with the title *Two Friends,* and also a novel; but all of them, so Grimm reported in the *Correspondance littéraire,* had been "universally hissed," and certainly Saint-Lambert's tale was an insipid and verbose piece. Diderot therefore wrote his story, also featuring two friends, as a kind of critique of Saint-Lambert's. His own "Two Friends" was to be a passionate but deliberately unsentimental story; a story not of tearful speech-making about friendship but of *unspoken* friendship; a study of the "natural man" not as virtuous exemplar but as criminal, or at least what conventional opinion branded as criminal.

It was also, though, an example of fiction as fraud. By agreement, Madame de Prunevaux sent it—that is to say the first part of the story, up to Olivier's death—to her "little brother" Naigeon (as she called him) as her own account of real-life events in the Bourbonne area. (Bourbonne was in the heart of smuggling country.) Naigeon, not a man much attuned to jokes, was duly taken in and asked to be told what had happened to Felix after his friend's death; and so this part, also, got written. Then finally, according to a favorite pattern with Diderot, further supplements were added, moving the focus away from Felix and Olivier to the margins of the story: to the process, a morally shabby one, by which the public gets to work on their reputations, and to general reflections on the nature of fiction and the three paths open to it.

The style of this story puzzled Diderot's friends, when they came read it. He was, in their eyes, a Shaftesburian enthusiast and sentimentalist, an inspired but prolix testifier to the Good and the True, above all *warm*. Indeed this remained his reputation with posterity, as when the nineteenth-century critic Barbey d'Aurevilly wrote of Grimm "hatching in his cold belly the burning egg that was Diderot." Thus it was hard for them to recognize him in this abrupt, incisive, and deliberately "cold" style. They thought it, on the whole, "detestable,"[4] and their reaction is significant. For it is precisely in the tension between the "warm" and the "cold," between the decency of the man of good will and the ruthlessness of genius, between the salon speechifier whom his friends saw and the skeptical self-observer, that the inspiration for Diderot's fiction lies. It took until the mid-nineteenth century, and the battles over "Realism" and Zolaesque "Naturalism," for this aspect of his fiction to come into focus.

In the same weeks or months that Diderot was writing "The Two Friends" he also composed "Conversation of a Father with His Children." This subtle work, at once affectionate reminiscence and philosophical apologue, explores the question of whether, in moral problems, the ultimate court of appeal should be public opinion and the "rules" or private ethical instinct. Diderot's father, a master cutler in Langres, was a man renowned for his piety, with a local reputation as a Solomon and settler of cases of conscience. He greatly disapproved of Denis's subversive and atheistical opinions, and the two quarreled violently on occasion; indeed Diderot senior once had Denis imprisoned in a monastery by *lettre de cachet*. It was thus a cause for bitter jealousy on the part of Denis's younger brother, Didier-Pierre, the "Abbé" of the "Conversation"—an orthodox, high-minded, and exceedingly self-righteous and tetchy character—that his father seemed actually to prefer the reprobate Denis. Denis, for his part, had a running quarrel with his brother, over tolerance and whether an atheist could be a good man, and he liked to raise this family quarrel, as he raised most things, to philosophical status. Thus he would sometimes disseminate his letters to his brother in the pages of the *Correspondance littéraire,* and once at least he addressed his brother over these issues in the preface to a book.

The method of the "Conversation" is, in its relaxed way, the multiple-perspective method that he often employed. As each new case of conscience is brought before Diderot senior at his fireside, the issue of public opinion versus private instinct is given a new twist and made to touch on different sympathies—the personal opinion of "MYSELF" being cunningly held back. All Diderot's fiction is concerned, in one way or another, with reconciling such intransigent opposites; and here a special mode of reconciliation is floated as a possibility, one made possible by affection. It is a mode one might call enlightened Pharisaism. Both "MYSELF" and his father think it good that certain attitudes should be held, but they do not want to hold them themselves: thus they wash their hands of the matter by wishing it on others. The final whispered exchange between "MYSELF" and his father is the key to the whole dialogue. "MY FATHER: 'I should not be too sorry if there were one or two in the town like you; but I should not live there if they all thought the same.'" "MYSELF," so Diderot's tone implies, would say exactly the same of his father.

"Supplement to Bougainville's *Voyage*" followed a year or so later and arose as a kind of afterthought to a review that Diderot had written, near the end of 1771, of the explorer Louis-Antoine de Bougainville's *Voyage Round the World.* His fictitious "Supplement" to Bougainville's narrative is a rich example of a certain supposititious or "foisting" technique that was one of Diderot's most original and fertile discoveries as writer. He takes over Bougainville's *Voyage,* shamelessly rewriting and falsifying it where necessary, and foists upon it the speeches and arguments that, for the "enlightened" reader, seem to cry out so urgently to be spoken.

About the same time, but we do not know exactly in what months, Diderot also wrote the stories "This Is Not a Story" and "On the Inconsistency of Public Opinion Regarding Our Private Actions"; and as he worked on these three stories ("story" is perhaps not the *mot juste* for the "Supplement," but it will do for the moment) they formed themselves into a connected trilogy. It is a fact which readers have been rather slow to recognize, or at least see the full significance of, though it is obvious when one is alerted to it, and indeed it was stated explicitly in the *Correspondance littéraire* when these three pieces appeared there in succession in the years 1773 and 1774. "The story that you are about to read is by M. Diderot," runs an editorial note to "This Is Not a Story." "It will be followed by several others by the same author. Not until the end of the final story will one see the moral and secret purpose underlying them." Of that "moral and secret purpose" I shall speak in a moment.

Meanwhile, though, I must try briefly to "place" Diderot as a novelist and story writer. I perhaps slightly exaggerated his isolation earlier, for there were two major influences on him, and they were both English. The first was Richardson, whom he discovered and was overwhelmed by in the year 1760, and the second, a little later, was Sterne; and what he made of these two conflicting influences, and how he reconciled them, is very striking. Indeed it suggests a theory about the rise of the novel rather different from the well-known ones of Ian Watt and Michael McKeon.[5]

One is inclined to view the early history of the novel from the point of view of the direction it eventually took. Thus—as represented by Ian Watt and Michael McKeon—Defoe, Swift, Richardson, and Fielding appear to be engaged in a joint enterprise. To a writer in the 1740s, however, it might rather have seemed that he or she was faced with a stark choice: a choice between, on the one hand, a conception of the novel as *deception,* as falsehood dressed up to look like truth and leaving a margin of possibility that it might in fact be truth, and, on the other hand, a conception of the novel as accepted illusion, illusion unambiguously acknowledged as such.

Now, plainly, any novel—like, say, *Tom Jones*—which has an elaborately contrived plot is bound to belong in the second category, the novel of accepted illusion. In the case of such a novel, the reader invites and expects the author to play entertaining games with him: to withhold essential information, drop clues that will only later reveal their significance, prepare peripateia, and so on; and over the years this familiar novelistic genre developed a whole conventional narrative rhythm, with dramas and lulls, suspenses and aftermaths, pauses for reminiscence and endings that are like deathbeds. It has been, and still is, a very fruitful genre; and for many years, through the genius of a Fielding, a Jane Austen, or a Turgenev, it came to seem almost like a synonym for the "novel" itself.

Nevertheless, at the beginning at least, there was another powerful and quite opposed vision of fiction, drawing inspiration from the possibility that a given fiction might not be a fiction at all but be true. This was how Defoe thought of the novel, and how Swift did, and, in his own way, how Richardson did; and one can see from the greatness of their achievement what a very rich approach it was. The primacy of Defoe, the inventor of an extraordinary new kind of verisimilitude and "perhaps the greatest liar who ever lived," is important here, and he was in this respect the direct inspiration for Swift. One remembers the extraordinary antics that Swift indulged in to sustain his anonymity at the time of *Gulliver.* What all this signifies is not that Swift was interested in hoaxing his readers in any literal sense, but rather that he had a vision of fiction as, in its very fiber, a synonym for fraud, deception, and counterfeiting.

Richardson, too, in his title pages and prefaces, went to great lengths to suggest that his novels were real-life documents, of which he was merely the "editor"; and his love of this device, as well as many other features of his work, places him squarely in the school of fiction as fraud or counterfeit.

Now, Diderot's masters in fiction were Richardson and Sterne: Richardson the counterfeiter and exponent of immediacy, hypnotic illusion, and vicarious participation, and Sterne the great dismantler of fictional illusion and disrupter of conventional author-reader relations. It is a fact which helps to revise our ideas of literary history. For over the years, and through the triumph of the Fieldingesque novel, Richardsonian "counterfeiting" has come to look naive, whereas Sternean disruption, as revived by twentieth-century writers, has come to seem avant-garde. Diderot, however, not only encompasses both of these two approaches but shows that they have deep affinities.

The point is clear in his first major novel, *The Nun,* which took its rise from an outrageous practical joke or hoax played by Diderot and some companions on a friend of theirs. This friend, the Marquis de Croismare, had deserted Paris for his country estate in Normandy, and Diderot and his associates, who missed his company, concocted a "horrible conspiracy" to cause him to return. The marquis, a most chivalrous man, had taken an interest a year or two earlier in the plight of a nun who was seeking to be released from her vows. Diderot and his confederates accordingly forged a letter to him, supposedly from this nun, informing him that she had escaped from her hated convent and was desperately in need of his help. The marquis replied; further letters from the "nun," of a compellingly Richardsonian kind, were composed; and de Croismare grew so intensely involved that his friends eventually felt obliged, out of decency, to kill the "nun" off.

In the course of this hoax, meanwhile, Diderot had become deeply involved with his own fictional creation. He had begun a letter from the nun, recounting her history for de Croismare's benefit, and it expanded under his hand into a complete novel. It was a novel à la Richardson and something else as well: a poignant and harrowing human narrative, exploiting the devices of hypnotic verisimilitude, and at the same time an exploration of the duplicities necessarily imposed on any first-person narrator—and especially one with so much to lose or gain from public opinion as the "Nun."

Diderot, in this first novel, had arrived at a bound at a powerfully original theory of fiction. We may state it quite concisely: fiction, for him, signified not a story, but the spectacle of somebody telling a story. The point is made in the opening lines of "This Is Not a Story."

> When one tells a story, there has to be someone to listen; and if the story runs to any length, it is rare for the storyteller not sometimes to be interrupted by his listener. That is why (if you were wondering) in the story which you are about to read (which is not a story, or if it is, then a bad one) I have introduced a personage who plays as it were the role of listener.

I shall come in a moment to the meaning of that paradoxical title "This Is Not a Story," but let me first expand on my phrase "the spectacle of somebody telling a story." How Diderot imagined this is made clearer in an "Essay on Painting" that he wrote in 1765. He is speaking there of composition in painting. A good composition, he says—as opposed to the frigid and artificial "contrasts" rigged up by academic painters—must represent an accommodation between a hundred independent energies and interests; and he draws an analogy from someone giving a reading.

> A man is reading something interesting to another man. Without either of them thinking about it, the reader adopts the posture most comfortable to him, and the listener does likewise. If Robbé[6] is reading, he will have the air of a zealot; he will not be looking at his text, his gaze will be far away. If it is I who am listening to him, I shall have a serious air. My right hand will seek out my chin and support my

drooping head; and my left hand will seek out the elbow of my right arm to support the weight of my head and of this arm. It is not thus that I should listen to Voltaire.

Add a third person to this scene, and he will submit to the same law as the two former; it is a combined system of three interests.

We may apply this metaphorically to Diderot's own fiction. The "system" of a fiction of his will involve at the very least three interacting, and possibly conflicting, "interests": those of the storyteller, a listener, and ourselves as readers. (Usually there will be more; there are so in several of the stories in the present collection.) It is, as one may see at once, a method very effective in suggesting the relativity of any fictional statement or thesis. It keeps alive the possibility that with other listeners or parties to the discourse the whole face of things might change. The novelist Michel Butor has put the point very well in an essay on "Diderot the Fatalist and His Masters," where he imagines a portraitist painting the spectacle of someone giving a reading.

> If the painter presented the person reading frontally, as if speaking directly to us, we should have no means of knowing that his posture was merely one among many possible ones; but if, on the contrary, he also includes a portrait of the primary spectator, he shows us by this that we constitute a third party on the scene; he gives an oblique view of the reader or reciter which allows us to see him in depth. . . . The depicted interlocutor gives us a parallax allowing us to calculate where we stand in regard to the speaker.[7]

What is also entailed, and again very important in Diderot's eyes, is that a fiction will never be finally separable from its matrix in real life, including the real life of the reader. He is continually concerned with the margins or "frames" of his stories. For instance, at the beginning of "This Is Not a Story," we come in at the tail end of someone else's piece of storytelling. Rather, we should say: he is concerned with unsettling any comfortable sense that his stories *are* safely "framed." Thus, in the first two stories in the present volume, he deliberately mixes up real-life personages (Gardeil, Mlle de la Chaux, and so on) with invented ones (Desroches, Mme de la Carlière, and others), and in the third, the "Supplement to Bougainville's *Voyage*," he puts invented sentiments into the mouths of characters in an already existing piece of writing, one already out there in the real world.

As for the paradox of a novelist asserting, "This is not a story," it can, we shall see if we reflect on it, have three possible meanings. It can mean, "This is not a *conventional* story, obeying the timeworn formulas of fiction-writers"; or it can mean, "This is not an invention, it actually happened"; or, thirdly, since a certain kind of fiction tries to make the reader say to himself, "This must be true; no one could have *invented* a detail like that," it can mean, "Trust no novelist, including the present one—for novelists love to *pretend* they are not writing a story." Diderot, who often comes back to the paradox (he does so repeatedly in *Jacques the Fatalist*), evidently requires us to understand it in all three senses, and for him it represents in summary form every possibility open to a fiction writer.

• • •

Such, then, was Diderot's very individual, very philosophical, theory of fiction; and it led him to find quite new and urgent things for fiction to say. This is certainly true of his trilogy, with which I have chosen to open this volume. Its central theme is announced in that meteorological discussion which frames the second and third of the stories. Two speakers are out walking on a foggy day, and the question that concerns them is whether, and if so when and by what means, the fog will clear and "points of blue" or starlight begin to pierce the murk. It is, as the reader gradually realizes, a most apt and subtle simile for the question already implicitly posed in "This Is Not a Story" and canvassed explicitly and passionately in "On the Inconsistency of Public Opinion": that is, have "reputation" and "public opinion" any validity at all? Three tragic love stories, three cases, have been presented to us. The first, that of the self-sacrificing Tanié, destroyed by the scheming Mme Reymer, is followed by its mirror reversal, that of the ruthless Gardeil and his gentle and hapless victim, Mlle de la Chaux; and then, in the next tale, we are presented with a case (that of the Chevalier Desroches and Mme de la Carlière) which subsumes these two previous tales and seems to be interpretable in the light of either or both, unsettling thereby any certainties that, as representatives of "public opinion," we readers may have arrived at.

The theme was adumbrated at the end of "This Is Not a Story." Were we right to pass such a final judgment on Gardeil as we were inclined to?

> . . . someone may perhaps tell me that it is much too hasty to pass judgment on a man on the strength of a single action; . . . that one may be inconstant in love, and even be quite unscrupulous when it comes to women, without being a total scoundrel or villain; . . . that there are enough men in our homes and our streets who richly deserve the name of rascal without inventing imaginary crimes which would multiply their number to infinity.

These doubts are silenced for the moment with a light question: would you, after all that has been said, and putting "your hand on your heart," choose Gardeil for your friend? They return, though, and with dizzying effect, in "On the Inconsistency of Public Opinion." Diderot lays a trap for his reader. When the reader comes to Mme de la Carlière's great oration to her lover on the eve of their marriage, he is almost bound to be carried away. "Give me the greatest mark of confidence that a self-respecting woman ever asked of a man of honor: *refuse me,* refuse me if you think I put too high a price on myself." These words, and the whole grandly conceived appeal, win the reader's heart. Thus, when exposed in the ensuing pages to a long and cruel reappraisal of Mme de la Carlière, the reader is really left wondering whether common ethics, or ordinary human sympathies, are fitted to cope with such issues at all.

Diderot's interlocutory method is, of course, crucial to the stories' effect. The "listener" in "This Is Not a Story" and the first of the two speakers in "On the Inconsistency" (we need not discuss here whether they are the same person) are conventional cynics, and as such they are contrasted with the altogether profounder skepticism of the storyteller himself. The "listener" generalizes with conventional misanthropy, and similarly the first speaker in "On the Inconsistency" jumps to trite conclusions (Desroches is a "madman") and foresees a trite and worldly-wise dénouement to Desroches' marriage, the kind of dénouement that novelists are expected to provide (Desroches will fall for the wiles of a designing woman), and he is rebuked for this conventionality by the second speaker. Cynicism, we see, is in itself a kind of security—one can always, as it were, *fall back* on cynicism—and the task of the narrator (as it is of Diderot himself) is to unsettle that security as much as any other.

The moral of "On the Inconsistency of Public Opinion" is clear. Mme de la Carlière has chosen to be judged by public opinion—that it so say, by a "tribunal" of friends and relations rather than by the impartial eye of God or conscience—and she must take the consequences. It is a poignant tale, for the consequences are dire. Public opinion, as it turns out (we see it again in "The Two Friends from Bourbonne") is a hopeless tribunal, weak, venal, and feather-headed, swayed by herd instinct, as the narrator's interlocutor admits to having been, and by instant emotion, as the reader convicts himself or herself of having been. If a just judgment on such as Desroches and Mme. de la Carlière is ever to emerge, it will be thanks not to the "public" but to some impersonal and weather-like natural process.

But, on the other hand, what other tribunal is there? No man is strong enough to content himself with his own good opinion, nor would he be right to. Virtue is a social matter; it is, anyway for an atheist, essentially a matter of other people's opinion. Hence the two opening stories of Diderot's trilogy seem to be posing a total dilemma. It remains for the concluding story, "Supplement to Bougainville's *Voyage*," to suggest that there may, after all, be a rational answer to that dilemma. It could be that the inconsistency of public opinion and the havoc and tragedy it brings are the fruit of something more basic—an error regarding sexual ethics, or the "attaching of moral ideas to certain physical actions which do not admit of them."

The author of the *Voyage* itself, the mathematician and explorer Louis-Antoine de Bougainville (1729–1814), began a circumnavigation of the globe at Nantes on November 15, 1766, and his ship *La Boudeuse* and its companion *L'Etoile* reached home again in the spring of 1769. His book came out in 1771, and, with its glowing report of the sexual freedom in Tahiti, it gave a great boost to what in Diderot's text is referred to as the "Tahiti fable." Bougainville was not in fact the originator of the fable, for one of his companions on the voyage, the naturalist Philibert Commerson, had already published an even more rapturous account of this sexual "utopia" in the South Seas. Bougainville was, moreover, not really a "primitivist" in the full sense: he gave a very bleak picture of the "state of nature" as exhibited by the Pecherais of Tierra del Fuego, and he was a fierce critic of Rousseau. His admirable book, however, was a godsend to Diderot, who saw it not only as intensely sympathetic but as ripe for appropriation.

Bougainville had described how, during the first joyous reception of himself and his crew in Tahiti, one old man, his host's father—a magnificent figure despite his great age, with scarcely a wrinkle on his sinewy body—stood aloof.

> He hardly seemed to notice our arrival. He withdrew as if unaware of our caresses, exhibiting neither fear, nor surprise, nor curiosity. Far from his taking part in the species of ecstasy the sight of us caused among his fellow islanders, his somber and reflective air seemed to proclaim a fear that his happy days, spent in the bosom of repose, would be marred by the arrival of a new race.[8]

The passage gave Diderot the cue for one of his most inspired feats of "supposititon," the great "Old Man's Farewell": an oration as magnificent in its eloquence as it is cunning in its dramatic irony.

Claude Lévi-Strauss has a striking passage in *Tristes tropiques* in which he attacks Diderot for being the crude "primitivist" and apologist of the "natural man" that Rousseau has been wrongly accused of being. Diderot's (or rather the Tahitian Orou's) "brief history of almost all our woe"—"Once there was a natural man: inside that man there was installed an artificial man, and within the cave a civil war began which lasted the whole of his life"—is, says Lévi-Strauss, absurd. "He who says 'man,' says 'language,' and he who says 'language' says 'society.' The Polynesians of Bougainville did not live in society any less than us."[9]

In a sense, of course, Lévi-Strauss is right, but this is to take Diderot's book for what it is not and to miss its elaborate ruses and ironies. Diderot's polemical strategy in this "Supplement" is really very complex, and, as with many of his best writings, it is actually a succession of supplements, designed to revise and sometimes to subvert one another.

At two points, above all, the reader finds a polemical trick has been played upon him or her. The first is a game played with utopian satire. The reader is drawn enjoyably into the "Erewhonian" reversal of values by which, in Diderot's Tahiti, chastity is considered a deep reproach, if not a crime, and it is the grossest failure of good manners on the Chaplain's part to refuse to sleep with his host Orou's daughters—or, for that matter, his wife. But then, as guest and host grow more intimate, Orou reveals a secret. This sexual Arcadianism is no mere utopian reversal of European mores but rather a cunning eugenic calculation. The European visitors, inferior as they are in almost all respects, possess one advantage, as the Tahitians have realized—a superior intelligence. Hence Tahitian wives and daughters are under orders to get themselves pregnant by the Europeans, to "harvest the seed of a race superior to our own." "We have extracted the sole profit that we could from you," says Orou to the Chaplain. "And I would have you know that, though we are savages, we too know how to calculate."

The second piece of subversion comes later, in the concluding conversation between "A" and "B." "B" begins to push the contrast between Europe and Tahiti to extremes, in a way that is not so much romantic-primitivist as misanthropic. As he is representing matters, humankind is faced with a choice between two evils: between a civilized life in which, through male chauvinism, property-mania, and social injustice, the sexual act becomes a source of infinite woe; and a savage life which is sunk in "mediocrity," benumbing indolence, and unenlightenment. With a final reductio ad absurdum he caricatures his position beyond all mistaking. He asserts that only two places on earth are suited to human beings: Tahiti, where they have the wisdom not to trouble their heads with enlightenment, and Venice, where they are too cowed to do so. His extravagance gives the game away, and we realize we have been the victims of one more polemical ploy.

There follows a palinode, expressing a sober and unfanatical view which we are safe in taking as Diderot's own. "So what shall we do?" asks "A"—to which "B" answers, "What we must do is to speak against insane laws until they are reformed, but in the meantime to obey then." In the "Supplement," as we realize, the doctrine that Diderot is underwriting is not primitivism at all, but a more cogent, serious, and humane one: that it is madness to create institutions that go against the grain of life and set humans at war with their own selves. It is a doctrine running through the whole of the trilogy; and, persuaded by his chastened tone, we are disposed to listen to the claim to which, all the time, the stories have been moving: that, if the fog of prejudice would clear, tragedies such as those that befell Gardeil, la Chaux, Desroches, and de la Carlière might simply prove unnecessary.

THIS IS NOT A STORY

When one tells a story, there has to be someone to listen; and if the story runs to any length, it is rare for the storyteller not sometimes to be interrupted by his listener. That is why (if you were wondering) in the story which you are about to read (which is not a story, or if it is, then a bad one) I have introduced a personage who plays as it were the role of listener. I will begin.

• • •

... So what do you think? — *I think that a subject as interesting as that ought to have been made thrilling; ought to be enough to keep the town amused for a month; ought to call for endless chewing over; ought to provoke a thousand disputes, twenty pamphlets at least, and several hundred verse-plays, on one side or the other. So, seeing that, with all the author's subtlety and learning and wit, his work did not stir us particularly, it must have been second-rate, terribly second-rate.* — Still, it seems to me to have given us a pleasant evening; and the reading has left us with... — *With what? A litany of shopworn anecdotes, telling us what everyone has known since the day of creation: that man and woman are two very mischievous creatures.* — All the same, you caught the infection and listened like the rest. — *Only because, for good or evil, one adopts the tone of the moment. When one enters a gathering, one customarily adjusts everything, even one's own features, at the door, to suit the company; one pretends to laugh when one is sad or to be sad when one is feeling like laughing; one is "knowing" about everyone and everything; the man of letters talks politics, and the politician talks metaphysics; the metaphysician talks ethics, the moralist talks finance, the financier talks belles-lettres or geometry. Rather than listen and hold one's tongue, everyone chatters about things they know nothing about and are bored, and bore others, out of stupid vanity or mere good manners.* — You seem to be in a bad mood. — *I usually am.* — It might be best if I kept my little story for another occasion. — *You mean, when I am not here?* — No, I don't mean that. — *Or you are afraid I will not be as kind to you, in private, as I would be in a crowded drawing room, with someone I didn't know.* — No, that's not the reason. — *Then be so good as to tell me what the reason is.* — It's because my little tale will not *prove* anything, any more than the one that has just bored you. — *Well, anyway, go ahead.* — No, no; you have had enough for today. — *Do you realize that, of all the ways people have of annoying me, yours is the one I detest most?* — And what is my way? — *Wanting to be entreated to do what you are dying to do anyway. So, my friend, I beg you, I implore you: go on and enjoy yourself.* — Enjoy myself! — *Begin, for God's sake, begin.* — I will try to be brief. — *That will do no harm.*

Here, a little out of malice, I coughed, I spat, I took out my handkerchief, I blew my nose, I opened my snuffbox, I took a pinch of snuff; and I heard my good friend mutter, "The story may be brief, but the preliminaries are certainly long." It crossed my mind to call a servant and pretend to send him on an errand, but I refrained; and I began:

This is not a story

It is a fact that there exist men who are truly good and women who are thoroughly wicked. — *We see it every day and sometimes without going out of our own front door. And so?* — And so? I once knew a beautiful woman from Alsace, so beautiful she made old men come running and halted young men in their tracks. — *And I knew her too; she was called Madame Reymer.* — Quite right; and a man called Tanié, who had just arrived from Nancy, fell madly in love with her. He did not have a penny. He was one of those poor wretches of children with too many brothers and sisters, who are driven from home by the harshness of their parents and cast themselves on the world, with no idea what will become of them, because instinct tells them at least they couldn't be worse off than they are. Tanié, being in love with Madame Reymer, and inspired by a passion which made him brave and glorified everything he did in his own eyes, cheerfully performed the most unpleasant and humblest of tasks to support his mistress. By day he worked at the docks, and in the evening he would beg in the streets. — *This was all very fine, but it could not last.* — So Tanié, tired of struggling against poverty, or rather of struggling to keep a charming woman in poverty when she was besieged by wealthy men, who wanted her to get rid of that good-for-nothing Tanié... — *As she would have done before the end of another fortnight, or at most a month.* — ... and accept their own rich offers—decided to leave her and seek his fortune abroad. He applies for, and obtains, a passage on a ship of the royal navy. The moment of departure arrives; he goes to bid Madame Reymer farewell. "My dearest," he says to her, "I must not take advantage of your tenderness any longer. I have made up my mind what to do, and I am leaving." "You are going away?" "Yes." "Where to?" "To the West Indies. You deserve a better fate, and I must not stand in your way any longer." — *The fine fellow!* — "And what is to become of me?" — *The false creature!* — "You are surrounded by suitors of all kinds. I release you from all your vows and promises. Make up your mind which suitor you like best and accept him: do it, I beg you." "Ah, Tanié, for you to suggest such a thing..." — *You can spare me Madame Reymer's charade; I know all about it, I can imagine it for myself.* — "Now that I am going away, I only ask one favor: do not make any commitment which separates us two forever. Swear it, my dearest. Wherever I am in the world, I shall indeed be in desperate straits if, once a year, I don't send you proof of my devotion. Do not cry. — *They all cry whenever it suits them.* — And do not try to stop me, it is self-reproach that has driven me to it and would do so later if not now." So Tanié goes to San Domingo. — *Just at the right moment for Madame Reymer and for himself.* — What do you know about it? — *I know, as surely as one can know anything, that when Tanié was urging her to choose a new protector, he had already been chosen.* — Very well! — *Go on with your story.* — Tanié was a man of intelligence, with a great talent for business. He soon made a name for himself. He became a member of the Sovereign Council of the Cape.[1] He distinguished himself there by his enlightened views and his sense of justice. He was not looking for a vast fortune; all he wanted was a modest income, and in the shortest possible time. Every year he sent part of his savings to Madame Reymer. Finally he returned... — *Nine or ten years later. No longer than that, I think.* — ... to present his mistress with a little purse, containing the fruits of his virtues and his labors. — *And luckily for Tanié it was when she had just got rid of the last of his successors* — The last? — *Yes.* — So there had been quite a number? — *Certainly. Do go on.* — But maybe I have nothing to tell you that you don't already know better than me? — *What does it matter? Go on all the same.* — Madam Reymer and Tanié lived in quite a pleasant apartment in the rue Sainte Marguerite, very near mine. I thought a lot of Tanié and was often in his house, which, if not exactly opulent, was certainly very comfortable and decent. — *I can confidently assure you, without consulting Madame Reymer's account book, that she had an income of more than fifteen thousand livres before Tanié's return.* — And she concealed it from him? — *Yes.* — Why? — *Because she was greedy and miserly!* — Greedy, maybe; but miserly! a courtesan miserly? After all, those two had lived together for five or six years in perfect camaraderie. — *Thanks to the extreme cunning of the one and the boundless trustfulness of the other.* — Oh, it is quite true, no shadow of a suspicion could enter a soul as pure as Tanié's. The only thing I did notice was that Madame Reymer had fairly quickly forgotten her onetime poverty; that she had become tormented by a love of wealth and luxury; that she thought it humiliating that a woman as beautiful as her should have to walk on her own two feet, — *Why did she not ride in a carriage?* — and that for her the glamour of vice concealed its baseness. That makes you laugh?... It was just about this time that Maurepas[2] had the idea of setting up a business-house in Russia. To succeed, the scheme needed a man of enterprise and intelligence. His eye fell on Tanié, whom he had employed on various important affairs during his sojourn at the Cape and had always acquitted himself very well. Tanié felt wretched to be singled out in this way; he was so contented with life, so happy just to be at his beautiful mistress's side and be loved, or at least believe himself loved. — *You put it very well.* — What could gold add to his happiness? Nothing. Nonetheless the Minister was insistent, a decision had to be taken, and Madame Reymer would have to be told about it all. I arrived at their house just at the end of the painful scene. Poor Tanié was in tears. "What is the matter, my friend?" I asked. Between sobs he replied, "It's that woman." Madame Reymer went on calmly with her embroidery. Tanié leaped to his feet and left the room. I remained behind with his mistress, who made no bones about what she called Tanié's "madness." She harped a great deal on their poverty. She argued her case with all the skill a subtle mind can use to cloak the sophistries of ambition. "After all, what does it amount to? To be away two or three more years at most." "It is a long time for a man you love, and who loves you as he does his own soul." "He, love me! If he did, could he hesitate a moment to do what I ask?" "But Madame, why don't you go with him?" "Oh, quite out of the question. Even he isn't mad enough to suggest such a thing. Doesn't he trust me?" "I have no idea." "Seeing that I waited for him for twelve years, he should be able to trust me for another three. Monsieur, it is the sort of chance that comes only once in a lifetime. I don't want him regretting some day that he didn't take it and, maybe, holding me to blame."

"Tanié will have no regrets, as long as he has the good fortune to please you." "You are very obliging. All the same, when I am an old woman, he will be glad enough to be rich. The mistake women make is never to think about the future. I am not like that...." The Minister was in Paris. It was only a step from the rue Sainte Marguerite to his residence. Tanié had gone there and accepted the post. He returned dry-eyed but with a heavy heart. "Madame," he said, "I have seen M. de Maurepas. He has my promise, and I shall go. I shall go, and you shall have your wish." Madame Reymer puts aside her needlework, rushes to Tanié, throws her arms round his neck, and covers him with kisses and endearments. "Ah, my friend!" she exclaimed, "now I can see you really love me!" Tanié replied coldly: "You want to be rich," — *She was rich, the slut, and ten times more than she deserved to be.* — "and so you shall be. Since it is gold that you love, we shall have to go and find you some." It was a Tuesday, and the Minister had told him he must leave by Friday at the latest. I went to bid him goodbye, just when he was struggling with himself and trying to tear himself from the arms of the beautiful, ignoble, and cruel Reymer. Never have I witnessed such confusion of mind, such despair, such agony. He was uttering not just a groan, but a continuous, unending wail. Madame Reymer was still in bed, and he was clutching one of her hands. He repeated, time after time: "Cruel woman! Cruelest of women! What more did you need than the comfortable means you already had and a friend, a lover, like me? I went to seek a fortune for her on the burning plains of America, now she wants me to seek another in the snows and ice of the North. My friend, I believe that woman is mad; and I am half mad too, but it terrifies me less to die than to make her unhappy.... You want me to leave you, and I shall leave you." He was kneeling at the side of her bed, his mouth glued to her hand and his face hidden in the bedclothes, which muffled his murmurs, making them all the more sad and frightening. The door opened, and he looked up with a start; it was the postilion, come to tell him the horses were harnessed and ready. He uttered a cry and hid his face in the bedclothes once more. After a moment of silence he got his feet. He said to his mistress, "Kiss me, Madame, kiss me just once more, for you will never see me again." His presentiment was all too well founded. He left; he arrived in St. Petersburg, and three days later he was struck down by fever; on the fourth he died. — *I knew all that.* — Perhaps you were one of Tanié's successors? — *Exactly. And she is the beautiful monster who helped to destroy me.* — Poor Tanié. — *Some people would say he was a fool.* — I wouldn't contradict them; but I would be hoping in my heart that fate would choose them a woman as beautiful and as contriving as Madame Reymer. — *You like your vengeances cruel.* — But then, if there are women who are very wicked and men who are very good, there are also very good women and very bad men; and what I am going to say now is no more a story than what has gone before. — *I am sure of it.*

• • •

Monsieur d'Hérouville.[3] — *The one who is still alive, who was Lieutenant-general of the King's armies, the one who married that charming creature Lolotte?* — The very same. — *He is a noble fellow, a friend to learning.* — And to the learned. He had been at work for a long time on a general history of war, through the centuries and among all the nations. — *It's a pretty large subject.* — To carry it out he had gathered talented young men round him, such as M. de Montucla,[4] who wrote a history of mathematics. — *Good lord! were there many of them, as able as that?* — Yes. The man named Gardeil,[5] the hero of the story I am about to tell, reckoned to be his equal or better. We shared a passion for studying Greek, and this began a friendship between Gardeil and me, one that time, our advice to each other, our taste for seclusion, and above all just being thrown together, turned into a considerable intimacy. — *You were living at the time in the rue de l'Estrapade.* — And he was living in the rue Saint Hyacinthe, and his mistress, Mademoiselle de la Chaux,[6] in the place Saint Michel. I call her by her own name, because the poor creature is no more, and because her life is one that all decent people must honor—one that those whom nature has blessed, or cursed, with even a fraction of such a feeling heart must think of with admiration, regrets, and tears. — *There was a catch in your voice. I do believe you are weeping.* — I seem still to see her great dark eyes, shining and gentle, and her touching voice still rings in my ears and troubles my heart. Charming creature! Unique creature! You are no more, it is twenty years since you are gone, but my heart still bleeds for you. — *You were in love with her?* — No. But oh, la Chaux! Oh Gardeil! you were both prodigies: you of womanly tenderness, and you of man's ingratitude. Mademoiselle de la Chaux came from a good family but left her home to throw herself into Gardeil's arms. Gardeil did not have a penny; she had a little property and sacrificed it entirely to Gardeil's needs and whims. She did not regret losing it, nor the loss of her good name; her lover was compensation for everything. — *So Gardeil was a charming, attractive fellow?* — Not in the very least: a surly, taciturn, sardonic little brute, dried-up and swarthy-complexioned and physically puny—even ugly, if a man with a face so full of intelligence can be called ugly. — *And this is the man who could turn the head of a charming young woman?* — Does that surprise you? — *Yes even now.* — You of all people? — *Yes.* — You have forgotten your affair with the Deschamps[7] woman and your terrible despair when she shut her door on you? — *Let's not talk about that. Go on with your story.* — I used to say to you, "So she is so beautiful?" and you would groan "No"; "Well then, wonderfully intelligent?" "She's an absolute idiot!" "You are attracted by her talents?" "She has only one." "And what is this rare, sublime, miraculous talent?" "To make me happier in her arms than I am in any other woman's." — *But what about Mademoiselle de la Chaux?* — Mademoiselle de la Chaux, with all her nobility and sensitivity, was promising herself—secretly, instinctively, unknowingly—the same happiness as you experienced, the happiness which made you say, "If that wretched, infamous woman insists on throwing me out, I shall take a pistol and blow my brains out in her hallway." Am I right? Did you say that, or didn't you? — *I said it, and to this day I don't know why I didn't go ahead and do it.* — Then you must agree. — *I will agree to anything you like.* — My friend, the wisest among us should bless himself not to have met the woman, whether beautiful or ugly, intelligent or a fool, who could have driven him mad and sent him to the asylum. Let us have pity for men, let us be chary of condemning them, let us look on our own past as so many moments stolen from the evil which pursues us; and let us never think without trembling of the violence of certain natural attractions, especially for warm natures and fiery imaginations. A stray spark falling on a barrel of gunpowder produces no more terrible effect, and the finger that will drop that fatal spark on you or me may already be raised.

M. d'Hérouville, being eager to finish his work, wore his helpers out. Gardeil's health suffered. To lighten his labors, Mademoiselle de la Chaux taught herself Hebrew and, while her lover rested, she would spend half the night construing and transcribing extracts from Hebrew authors. Then came the time to ransack the Greeks. She hastened to perfect her Greek, having already some smattering of it, and while Gardeil slept she would be busy translating and copying from Xenophon and Thucydides. To her knowledge of Greek and Hebrew she added Italian and English. She was proficient enough in English to translate the first essays in metaphysics by Hume, a work in which the difficulty of the subject matter added enormously to the difficulties of language. When exhausted by research, she would occupy herself engraving music. If she saw her lover falling into depression, she would sing to him. I am not exaggerating all this. I can call to witness M. le Camus,[8] a doctor friend of hers, who consoled her in her troubles and helped her in her poverty: a man who did her endless good turns, pursued her to her miserable garret when poverty drove her there, and closed her eyes when she died. — But I am forgetting one of her very first troubles, the persecution she suffered for so long from her family, who resented all the scandal caused by her love affair. They used every means, both truth and lies, to threaten her liberty. Her relations and their priests chased her from district to district, from house to house, and for several years they forced her to live all alone and in hiding. She would spend her days working for Gardeil. We would come to see her in the evening, and at the sight of her lover all her misery, all her anxiety vanished. — *To be young, timid, and full of feeling and suffer such misfortunes!* — She was happy. — *Happy!* — Yes, and went on being so till Gardeil proved ungrateful. — *But that cannot have happened. So many rare qualities, so many loving deeds, so many sacrifices of every kind: their reward could not have been ingratitude!* — You are wrong, Gardeil was not grateful. One day Mademoiselle de la Chaux found herself alone in the world, without reputation, without money, without support. Not quite true: she still had me, for the time being, and Doctor le Camus she would always have. — *Oh men! men!* — Who do you mean? — *Gardeil.* — You are thinking of the wicked man and do not notice the decent man by his side. On that day of sorrow and despair she came hurrying to me. It was morning. She was pale as death. She had only learned her fate the night before, yet her appearance suggested long sufferings. She was not weeping, but one could see she had wept a great deal. She threw herself into a chair. She did not speak, she was incapable of speaking; she held out her arms to me, uttering groans. "What's the matter?" I asked her. "Is he dead?" "Worse, he does not love me any more. He means to leave me." "Then leave him yourself." "I cannot. I can see him, I can hear him, and my eyes are full of tears." "He doesn't love you any more?" "No." "He wants to leave you?" "He does, he does. And after all I have done! Monsieur, I am in a daze. Have pity on me. Do not desert me, above all do not you desert me too!" Uttering these words she clutched my arm and squeezed it violently, as if people were trying to drag her away. "Do not be afraid, Madame!" "I am afraid of no one but myself." "What can be done for you?" "First of all, save me from myself. He has stopped loving me, I weary him, I get on his nerves, I bore him, he hates me, he is deserting me, he is going to leave me, to leave me!" These words, twice spoken, were followed by deep silence, and that in turn by outbursts of convulsive laughter, a thousand times more alarming than accents of despair or a death rattle. Then tears, outcries, inarticulate words, eyes raised to heaven, trembling lips: a torrent of grief which had to be left to run its course. I let it do so and did not try to reason with her till sorrow had left her stupefied and broken. Then I tried again. "So he hates you and means to leave you? But who says so?" "He says so himself." "Come, Mademoiselle, a little hope, a little courage: he is not a monster." "You don't know him, you will never know him. He is a monster, the greatest monster there is or ever was." "I cannot believe that." "You will see." "Is he in love with somebody else?" "No." "Have you given him any reason for jealousy? Have you crossed him in any way?" "None, none." "Where does the trouble lie then?" "In my being useless to him. I have no money left, and I am no good to him any more. It's that, and his ambition—for he has always been ambitious—and my losing my health and my looks, through all that work and suffering; and just boredom, and disgust." "You could give up being lovers and remain friends." "No, he cannot bear me; my presence is a burden to him, the very sight of me upsets and distresses him. If you only knew what he said to me: that if he had to spend twenty-four hours shut up with me, he would throw himself out of the window." "But those feelings of his can hardly have sprung up overnight?" "How can I tell? He has always been so scornful, so indifferent, so cold. It is hard to see to the bottom of such souls, and one is afraid of what one may read there, since it may be one's own death sentence. But anyway, he delivered the sentence, and with such brutality!" "It is all beyond me." "I have a favor to ask of you. It is why I came. Will you grant me it?" "Yes," I said, "anything whatever." "It is this. He respects you, and you know how much he owes to me; he may perhaps blush to show himself to you as he really is. Yes, I don't think he has the effrontery or the strength of mind. I am only a woman, you are a man. A just, high-minded, tender-hearted man commands respect; you will impose it on him. Give me your arm and do not refuse to come with me. I want to speak to him in front of you. Who knows what effect my unhappiness and your presence may have on him? Will you come?" "With all the will in the world." — *Her unhappiness and your presence: much good they will do! Disgust, and losing desire for a woman, is a terrible thing in love.* — I sent for a sedan chair, for she was scarcely in a condition to walk. We arrived at Gardeil's lodgings: he was in that great new house in the rue Hyacinthe, the only big one on that side, as you enter it from the place Saint Michel. The porters stopped and opened the chair door. I waited, but she did not get out. I looked inside and saw she was trembling from head to foot: her teeth chattered like a fever patient's, her knees were knocking together. "One moment, Monsieur," she said. "I beg your pardon, I beg your pardon, I cannot... What could I possibly do there?... I have troubled you for nothing, I am sorry, I beg your pardon." Meanwhile I offered my arm. She took it, tried to get up, and could not. "One moment more," she said. "It must upset you to see me like this." At last she composed herself a little and got out, murmuring: "I have to do it. I have to see him! What will become of me? Perhaps I shall die." So there the two of us were, crossing the courtyard, outside Gardeil's door, and then right inside his study. He was at his desk in nightcap and dressing gown. He waved to me and went on with what he was writing. Then he came over to me, saying, "You must agree, Monsieur, women are very inconvenient creatures; I offer you a thousand apologies for Mademoiselle's strange behavior." Then, addressing the poor woman herself, by now more dead than alive, he said: "Mademoiselle, what do you want of me? I seems to me that, after the perfectly clear and precise explanation I gave you, matters between us should be at an end. I said to you that I no longer loved you. I said it when we were alone, but it appears you want me to repeat it in front of Monsieur. Very well. Mademoiselle, I do not love you any longer; love is a feeling extinct in my heart, so far as you are concerned—and, I might add, if it is any consolation, so far as any other woman is concerned." "But why, why do you not love me any more?" "I have no idea. All I know is, I began to love you without knowing why and now know perfectly well that my passion can never return. It's an infection I have thrown off and of which, to my best belief and satisfaction, I am completely cured." "What have I done wrong?" "Nothing." "Have you some secret objection to my conduct?" "None in the least. You have been the most faithful, most tender, most high-minded woman a man could ask for." "Have I failed to do something I could have done?" "Nothing!" "Did I not give up my family for you?" "Quite true." "And my fortune." "Regrettably, yes." "And my health?" "Perhaps." "And my honor, my reputation, my peace of mind?" "Whatever you please." "I am hateful to you?" "It's an unpleasant thing to have to say, and an unpleasant thing to hear, but that is the case, and I have to agree." "I am hateful to him!" "It is what I feel, and not a feeling I am proud of." "Hateful to him! Ah, my God!" At these words a mortal pallor spread over her features; her lips went white; drops of cold sweat stood out on her cheeks, mingling with tears; her eyes were tight shut, her teeth clenched, her head thrown back on the chair. All her limbs were trembling, and this trembling was followed by a swoon which seemed like the end she had earlier foreseen. It lasted long enough to frighten me. I took off her cloak, undid the strings of her dress and loosened her skirts, and threw some drops of cold water on her face. Her eyes half opened and she gave a low murmur; she was trying to say "... hateful to him" but could only manage the last syllable. Then she uttered a piercing cry, her eyelids closed, and she was unconscious again. Gardeil sat coolly in his chair, his elbow on the desk and his head in his hand, and looked on without emotion, leaving me to cope. I said from time to time: "Monsieur, she is dying, we must get help," to which he replied, with a smile and a shrug, "It takes more than that to kill a woman. It's nothing, it will soon be over. You don't know women; they can make their bodies do whatever they want." "I tell you she is dying," I repeated. And in fact her body seemed quite lifeless; it slipped off the chair and would have fallen on the floor, to one side or the other, if I had not held her. Meanwhile Gardeil had suddenly got to his feet and paced up and down the room, exclaiming impatiently and angrily: "I could have done without this revolting scene. Let us hope at least it's the last. Who the devil does the creature mean to blame? I used to love her, and beating my head against the wall will not alter that one way or the other. I don't love her any longer; she knows this by now, or she will never know it. It's all there is to say." "No, Monsieur, it's not all there is to say. What? You think a decent man can strip a woman of everything she has and then just leave her?" "What do you want me to do, I'm as much a beggar as she is." "What do I want you to do? I want you to join your poverty to hers, the poverty you have reduced her to." "It's all very well for you to talk. It would do her no good, and it would do me a lot of harm." "Would you behave the same way with a friend who had sacrificed everything to you?" "A friend! I don't have much faith in friends; and as for passion, this experience has taught me to have no faith in it at all. I wish I had learned it sooner." "And that unfortunate woman must pay for the mistake of your heart?" "Well, who is to say but that a month or a day later I should be suffering, and even more cruelly, from a mistake of hers?" "Who is to say? Why, everything she has done for you, and the state you see her in, say so." "Everything she has done for me! Oh my God, it's been well paid for already, by the wasting of my time!" "Monsieur Gardeil, can you compare this precious time of yours with all the priceless things of which you have robbed her?" "I have done nothing in life; I am nothing; I am thirty years old and the time has come, or it never will be come, to think of myself and to value all that other stupid nonsense as it deserves." In the meantime the poor woman had revived a little. Hearing Gardeil's last words she exclaimed: "What is that about wasting his time? I learned four languages to lighten his labor; I read a thousand books; I wrote, translated, copied night and day. I wore myself out, ruined my eyesight, consumed my blood. I have contracted a hateful disease that I may never be cured of. Do you want to know the reason for this disgust of his? He doesn't dare admit it, but you shall know it." On the instant she snatched off her *fichu,* pulled one of her arms out of her dress, and showed me her bare shoulder, covered with a great red patch of skin rash. "There you see it, the reason for his change," she said. "You see there the effect of my sleepless nights. He would arrive in the morning with great rolls of parchment. 'M. d'Hérouville is in a great hurry to know what is in these,' he would say. 'It needs to be done by tomorrow.' And it was."

At this moment we heard footsteps approaching outside. It was a servant, to tell us that M. d'Hérouville was on his way. Gardeil went pale. I advised Mademoiselle de la Chaux to dress and leave. "No," she said, "I shall stay, I want to show this base wretch up for what he is. I shall wait for M. d'Hérouville and speak to him." "What good will that do you?" "None," she sighed, "you are quite right." "You would regret it by tomorrow. Leave him to enjoy the fruits of crime in peace. It will be a fit vengeance for you." "But will it be fit for him? Don't you see that that man is... Monsieur, we must go this instant... I cannot answer for what I might do or I might say!" She hastily rearranged her clothes and shot from Gardeil's study like an arrow; I followed and heard the door slammed loudly behind us. Later I learned that the porter had had instructions to keep her out. I took her back to her lodgings, where I found Doctor le Camus waiting. The passion he nursed for that young woman was not so different from hers for Gardeil. I told him of our visit, to his visible anger, sorrow, and indignation. — *But it was not too hard to detect from his face that the failure of your mission did not altogether displease him?* — That is true. — *Mankind is like that; no better than that.* — The result of the break with Gardeil was a violent illness, during which the good, the noble, the tenderhearted, the considerate Doctor lavished care on her that he would not have given to the grandest lady in France. He came three times, four times, a day. As long as there was any danger, he slept in her bedroom, on a truckle bed. An illness can actually be a boon in times of very great distress. — *By throwing us back on ourselves it takes our mind off others; and then, it is an excuse to give way to our unhappiness without shame.* — A true remark, which, however, did not apply in the case of Mademoiselle de la Chaux.

During her convalescence we planned how she should occupy her time. She had intelligence, imagination, taste, and knowledge—more than enough to have earned her a seat in the Academy of Inscriptions. She had so often listened to us philosophizing that she was at home with the most abstract questions, and her first literary undertaking was a translation of the early work of Hume.[9] I was to revise it, but in fact there was very little for me to revise. The translation was printed in Holland and was very well received.

My *Letter on the Deaf and Dumb* came out at about the same time, and some ingenious objections that she made to it provoked me to write a further *Letter* on the subject, which I dedicated to her and is not the worst of my productions.

Mademoiselle de la Chaux had recovered her spirits a little. The Doctor used sometimes to invite us to a meal, and those dinners were by no means gloomy affairs. Since the defection of Gardeil, le Camus's passion had made prodigious progress. One day at his table, at dessert, he was discussing it himself, with all the good taste, the sensibility, the naiveté of a child and all the acuteness of a profound thinker, and she made him a reply. Its frankness pleased me infinitely, though it may not please others. "Doctor," she said, "no one could possibly feel more regard for you than I do. You have loaded me with kindnesses, and I would be as black a monster as the one of the rue Hyacinthe if I were not full of the intensest gratitude. Your way of thinking could not delight me more; you speak to me about your passion with so much delicacy and grace that, I really think, I should be sorry if you stopped. The mere idea of losing your company or your friendship is enough to make me miserable. You are a man of goodwill if ever there was one. The goodness and gentleness of your character are incomparable. I do not think that a human heart could fall into better hands. I preach to my own heart in your favor from morning till night; but it no use preaching to the deaf, and it gets me nowhere. Meanwhile you are unhappy, and this distresses me cruelly. I know no one more deserving than you of the happiness you ask for, and I can think of nothing I would not dare to do to make you happy. I would risk everything, everything without exception. Doctor, I would...! Yes, I would go as far as bed, even that. Do you want to go to bed with me? You have only to ask. That is all that I can do for you; but you want to be loved, and that is not in my power." The Doctor listened to her, took her hand, kissed it, and bathed it with tears, and as for myself, I did not know whether to laugh or to weep. Mademoiselle de la Chaux knew her Doctor friend well, and next day, when I said to her "What would have happened if the Doctor had taken you at your word?" she replied, "I would have kept my promise. But it could never have happened. My offers were not of a kind a man like him could accept." — *Why not? I have a feeling that, if I had been in the Doctor's place, I would have hoped that the rest would come later.* — Yes, but if it had been you and not him, Mademoiselle de la Chaux would not have made the offer.

The Hume translation had not earned her very much. The Dutch print whatever you like, so long as they don't have to pay.

— And a good thing for us. For, considering how free thought is stifled here, if it entered their mind to pay authors, the whole book trade would be lost to their country. — So we advised her now to try writing a work of entertainment, which might gain her more reputation and profit. She worked for four or five months and at the end brought me a little historical tale entitled "The Three Favorites." It was light in touch and engaging—also sly, though she did not realize this herself, being incapable of malice. It was full of touches people would apply to the King's mistress, the Marquise de Pompadour,[10] and I did not disguise from her that, even if she softened or suppressed them, her work would still be bound to get her into trouble; she would have spoiled her work, and all to no good purpose.

She saw the truth of what I said, and it was another blow for her. The good Doctor looked after her needs, but she accepted as little as she could from him, being unwilling to reward him in the way he might have hoped. Besides, at this period, the Doctor was by no means a rich man, nor was he cut out to become one. From time to time she would take out her manuscript and would say to me sadly: "So there is nothing to be done with it, and it will have to stay in the drawer?" Then I gave her some strange advice. It was to send the work to Madame de Pompadour herself, with a little covering note explaining why she had sent it. The idea appealed to her. She wrote the Marquise a letter which was charming in every way but above all in its note of frankness, which made it hard to resist. Two or three months passed without any word, and she was coming to the conclusion that the scheme had been a failure, when a highly distinguished-looking gentleman called upon her with the Marquise's reply. It praised her work as highly as it deserved, thanked her for sacrificing it, and acknowledged its home truths. The Marquise, it conveyed, was not offended. She invited the author to come to Versailles, where she would meet "a grateful woman, who was eager to do her such services as lay in her power." The envoy, as he left Mademoiselle de la Chaux's lodgings, discreetly deposited a roll of fifty *louis* on the mantelpiece.

The Doctor and I urged her to take advantage of Madame de Pompadour's goodwill; but we were dealing with a young woman whose modesty and timidity were quite as great as her merit. How could she present herself at Court in rags? The Doctor quickly solved that difficulty; but after clothes there came other excuses, and then more excuses. From day to day the journey to Versailles was put off till it would hardly have been decent to go. Indeed we had even ceased to talk about it, when the same emissary returned with a second letter, full of the most delicate reproaches, and with another gratuity of the same amount, offered in the same tactful way. This generous action of Madame de Pompadour's is not generally known. I spoke of it to M. Colin, her private secretary and distributor of her secret charities. He had not heard of it, and I like to imagine it is not the only such good deed which went unknown with her to the grave.

So in this way, Mademoiselle de la Chaux twice missed the chance to escape penury.

After this she moved to the outskirts of Paris, and I quite lost sight of her. From what I have learned of the rest of her life, it was a catalog of miseries, illness, and poverty. The doors of her family home remained resolutely closed to her. She appealed in vain to those reverend wearers of the cloth who had persecuted her with such zeal. — *All according to the rules.* — Only the Doctor did not desert her. She died on straw in a garret. Meanwhile the little tiger of the rue Hyacinthe, the only lover she had ever had, practiced medicine at Montpellier or at Toulouse and earned great prosperity, a well-deserved reputation as a man of talent and a quite undeserved reputation as a gentleman. — *And that too is, more or less, according to the rules. Given a good and honorable Tanié, Providence assigns him to a Reymer. Given a good and honorable de la Chaux, and she will be bestowed on a Gardeil, so that all shall be as it should be.*

But someone may perhaps tell me that it is much too hasty to pass judgment on a man on the strength of a single action; that with a rule as severe as that there would be fewer decent people left on earth than the Gospels admit to Heaven; that one may be inconstant in love, and even be quite unscrupulous when it comes to women, without being a total scoundrel or villain; that no one can stifle a passion when it begins to rage, or keep it burning when the flame goes out; that there are enough men in our homes and our streets who richly deserve the name of rascal without inventing imaginary crimes which would multiply their number to infinity. Someone will ask me whether I have never betrayed, deceived, or deserted a woman without good cause. If I replied to these questions, there would then be a reply to my reply, and the dispute would go on till Judgment Day. But put your hand on your heart and tell me, Monsieur the apologist of deceivers and betrayers, if you would choose the Doctor of Toulouse for your friend. You hesitate? I have my answer; and hereupon I pray God to keep in his holy protection any woman you choose to make your addresses to.

ON THE INCONSISTENCY OF PUBLIC OPINION REGARDING OUR PRIVATE ACTIONS

Shall we turn back? — It is still quite early. — *Do you see those clouds?* — Don't be afraid; they will disappear of their own accord, without the help of the slightest puff of wind. — *You think so?* — I have often noticed it in summer and hot weather. The lowest part of the atmosphere, relieved of its moisture by turning into rain, can reabsorb some of the thick vapor veiling the sky. The mass of this vapor will distribute itself more or less uniformly throughout the whole mass of air, and by that even distribution or combination, whichever you like to call it, the atmosphere becomes transparent and clear. It is one of our laboratory experiments conducted on the grand scale over our heads. Within a few hours, points of blue will begin to pierce the thinning clouds. The clouds will thin more and more. The points of blue will multiply and spread. Soon you will wonder what has happened to the black crape which so frightened you, and you will be surprised and pleased by the limpidity of the air, the serenity of the sky, and the beauty of the day. — *What you say is true! While you were talking I was watching, and the phenomenon seemed to proceed exactly according to your instructions.* — This phenomenon is simply a kind of dissolution of water by air. — *As the vapor which clouds the outside of a tumbler when one fills it with iced water is merely a species of precipitation.* — And those enormous balloons which float or hang suspended in the atmosphere are simply a superabundance of water which the saturated air cannot dissolve. — *They stay there like pieces of sugar at the bottom of a coffee cup, when the coffee can absorb no more.* — Yes, well done. — *And so you promise, on our return...* — As starry a vault as you have ever seen. — *As we are going to continue our walk, could you tell me, for you know all the regular visitors here, who that tall, dried-up, melancholy looking individual is who sat quite silent and who stayed on alone in the salon when the rest of the company dispersed?* — He is a man whose unhappiness I have a particular respect for. — *And what is his name?* — The Chevalier Desroches. — *Is he the Desroches who inherited a great fortune when his miser of a father died: the man who became so famous for his dissipation and his love affairs and all the different roles in life he played?* — Yes, that's him. — *That madman always in some new disguise: first in a cassock, then in a* Palais de Justice *robe, then in military uniform?* — The same poor madman. — *How changed he is!* — His life has been a tissue of strange events. There can have been few unluckier victims of the whims of fate and the rash judgments of mankind. When he left the church for the law his family made a great to-do; and the idiot Public, always on the side of fathers against children, barked and brayed as one man. — *And there was some fuss again, was there not, when he deserted the law for the army?* — Yes, and what had he done? A bold deed, a deed either of us would have been proud of, though it earned him the name of the craziest character in the world. Are you surprised that the shameless gossip of that rabble should bother me and upset me and put me in a rage? — *Upon my word, I took the same view of Desroches as everyone else.* — And that is how, by mindless repetition, the word gets passed from mouth to mouth, and a man of distinction passes for a dull clod, a man of intelligence for an idiot, a man of principle for a rascal, a brave man for a rash fool—and the other way round too. No, whether they are praising or blaming, we mustn't let those useless chatterers influence our own conduct. Listen to this, for God's sake, and die of shame! Desroches becomes a *conseiller* in *Parlement* as a very young man; fortune favors him, and he is soon admitted to the *Grand' Chambre*;[1] his turn comes round as a judge-advocate in the criminal court, and on the strength of a judgment of his a wrongdoer is sentenced to the extreme penalty. It is a custom that on the day of execution those who pronounced the sentence should be present in the Hôtel de Ville to receive the victim's last requests—should he make any, as was the case here. It was winter. Desroches and his colleague were sitting by the fire when word came that the victim had arrived. He was brought in on a mattress, his body mangled by torture, but he managed to raise himself as he entered and, with eyes toward heaven, exclaimed, "Almighty God, your judgments are just!" There he was, on his mattress, right at Desroches' feet. "So, Monsieur!" he cried to Desroches in a loud voice. "You condemned me, and I am guilty of the crime I am accused of; yes, I confess it. All the same, you know nothing, nothing at all..." And he went over the whole legal process step by step, showing, as clear as daylight, that there had been no substance in the proofs and no justice in the sentence. Desroches, seized with a mortal trembling, gets to his feet, tears off his magistrate's robe, and renounces forever the perilous profession of pronouncing upon men's lives. And this is the man they call mad! A man with self-knowledge, a man afraid to defile the garb of cleric by loose morals or to find himself, one day, stained with an innocent man's blood. — *The truth is, we didn't know all this.* — The truth is, if one doesn't know things, one should hold one's tongue. — *But that means distrusting oneself.* — And what harm would that do? — *And distrusting twenty people one respects in favor of someone one does not know at all.* — Well, Monsieur! I don't ask for so much caution in doing good. But when it's a matter of evil...! We had better drop the subject. You are distracting me from my story and making me angry... Meanwhile Desroches was in need of a career. So he bought a regiment. — *That is to say, he exchanged the profession of condemning his fellow men to death for the simpler one of just killing them.* — I am surprised you find it a joking matter. — *Well, there we are! You are sad, and I am cheerful.* — It's the rest of his story that shows us what the public and its chatter are really worth. — *I should be glad to hear it, if you are willing.* — It's a long story. — *So much the better.* — Desroches fought in the campaign of 1745 and acquitted himself well. Having escaped the dangers of war and two hundred thousand bullets, he contrived to get his leg broken by a skittish horse. It happened ten or fifteen leagues from the country house he had planned to use for winter quarters. God knows what the wits made of his accident. — *There are certain people it becomes a sort of habit to laugh at and who get pity from nobody.* — A man who has broken his leg; so amusing! Well, my fine laughers-for-no-good-reason, enjoy your laugh; but let me tell you something, it might have been better for Desroches to be taken off by a cannonball or to lie on the battlefield with a bayonet through his belly. His accident had taken place in a wretched little village where the only bearable places to stay were the presbytery or the château. They took him to the château, which belonged to the local lady of the manor, a young widow named Madame de la Carlière. — *Who has not heard speak of Mme de la Carlière? Who has not heard of her kindness and tolerance toward a jealous old husband to whom she had been sacrificed by her parents' greed at the age of fourteen?* — At the age when one takes the most serious decision in life, for the privilege of wearing rouge and having one's hair curled. Mme de la Carlière behaved toward her first husband with the greatest tact and decorum. — *I will believe it, if you tell me so.* — She took the Chevalier Desroches in and looked after him with all possible kindness. She was needed in town; but despite her business there, and despite the continual autumn rains, which swelled the waters of the nearby Marne and threatened to make her a total prisoner in the château, she stayed on in the country until Desroches was completely cured.... So now he is cured. Now he is sitting beside Mme de la Carlière in a carriage en route for Paris and is bound by gratitude, and by an even sweeter sentiment, to this young, rich, and beautiful Sister of Mercy. — *It is quite true; she was a ravishing creature. Her beauty would cause a stir whenever she entered a theater.* — That is where you saw her? — *Exactly.* — Several times during their intimacy, which lasted some years, the amorous Chevalier, to whom Mme de la Carlière was by no means indifferent, proposed marriage to her; but the memory, still fresh, of her sufferings with her tyrant of a husband, and even more the Chevalier's own reputation as a trifler and breaker of hearts, frightened Mme de la Carlière, who had no faith in such men's conversion. She was at this time involved in a lawsuit with her husband's heirs. — *No doubt this was much discussed between them?* — Very frequently, and from all points of view. You can imagine whether Desroches, who still had a number of friends in the magistracy, let the grass grow over Mme de la Carlière's case. — *Or whether she was grateful.* — He was continually knocking on the Judges' doors. — *And what was a nice touch, so I hear, was that, though his fracture had been healed for many months, he never visited them without a splint; he claimed that the splint made his appeals more touching. It is true, he wore it sometimes on one leg and sometimes on the other, and people would notice.* — So that to distinguish him from a relative of the same name he became known as "Desroches of the Splint." Nevertheless, with the aid of a just cause and the Chevalier's pathetic splint, Mme de la Carlière won her case. — *And became Madame Desroches* en titre? — What a rate you go at! You cannot be bothered with petty details, and I will spare you them. They had come to an understanding and were on the eve of their wedding, when, after an elaborate formal meal, and in the midst of a large circle, the members of their two families and some of their friends, Mme de la Carlière addressed the Chevalier in stately and solemn fashion. "Monsieur Desroches," she said, "listen to me. Today we are free of one another, tomorrow we shall be so no longer and I shall be the mistress of your happiness and you the master of mine. I have been thinking about this very seriously; have the goodness to do likewise. If you can detect in yourself the same bent toward inconstancy as in the past; if I am not enough to fulfill all your desires; do not take your marriage vows, I beg it for your own sake and for mine. Remember that the less I felt I deserved neglect, the more intensely I would resent it. I have vanity, a great deal of vanity. I do not know how to hate, but no one knows better than I how to despise, and once I despise there is no going back. Tomorrow, at the foot of the altar, you will swear to belong to me and to no one but me. Search your soul, question your heart, while there is still time. Consider that my life hangs on it. Monsieur, I am easily wounded, and my soul's wounds do not grow scars, they bleed forever. I shall not complain, because complaining, which is always useless, ends by making an evil worse, and because pity is a sentiment which degrades the person who provokes it. I shall lock my grief up in my heart, and I shall die of it. Chevalier, I am about to abandon my person and my property to you, to sacrifice my wishes and my whims to you; you will be everything in the world to me, and I must be everything in the world to you, I cannot be content with less. I am, I believe, the sole person for you at the moment, and you certainly are so for me; but is very possible we shall meet—in your case a more lovable woman, in mine a man who at least seems more lovable. If superiority of merit, real or presumed, is to justify infidelity, there is an end to morality. I have moral standards, I am glad to have them, I want you to have them. My claim to own you, and to own you without reserve, is based on all imaginable sacrifices. These are my rights, these are my titles, and I do not mean to concede an iota of them. If you fail me, I shall do my best to make you appear, in the judgment of all right-thinking people and even in your own, not just a philanderer but the worst of all ingrates. I shall accept the same reproach if I do not respond to your considerateness, your tenderness, your care for me, even beyond your hopes. I discovered what I was capable of beside a husband who did not make a wife's duties easy or agreeable. So see if you have any reason to distrust yourself. Speak to me, Chevalier, speak to me clearly: either I become your wife, or I remain your friend, the choice is not such a cruel one. My friend, my dear friend, I beg you, do not cause me to detest and flee the father of my children or, in an access of despair, to rebuff their innocent caresses. Let me, all through life, and with new pleasure each time, rediscover you in them and rejoice to have been their mother. Give me the greatest mark of confidence that a self-respecting woman ever asked of a man of honor: *refuse me,* refuse me if you think I put too high a price on myself. Far from being offended, I shall throw my arms round your neck; and the love of all the women you ever charmed, and all the pretty speeches you ever made them, will never have earned you a kiss so sweet, so sincere, as the one earned by frankness on your part and by gratitude on mine. — *I believe I once heard a very funny takeoff of this speech.* — No doubt from some dear friend of Mme de la Carlière's? — *Good lord, I remember now; you are quite right.* — And is that not enough to drive a man to the depths of the forest, away from the well-dressed vermin for whom nothing is sacred? That's what it will mean. It will come to that, I swear it; I will have to go.... The party begun with smiles ended in tears. Desroches threw himself at Mme de la Carlière's knees. He poured forth noble and tender protestations, omitted nothing which could either aggravate or excuse his past conduct, painted the whole contrast between Mme de la Carlière and the women he had loved and left and drew from this just and flattering comparison reasons to reassure her—reasons to reassure himself too—against what was after all only a modish caprice, a mere youthful frivolity, a vice of the age in general rather than of his own. He said nothing that he did not mean, or that he was not promising himself to do. Mme de la Carlière gazed, listened, strove to discern the man behind the words and the gestures, and interpreted everything in his favor. — *Why not, if it was all sincere?* — She had let him take one of her hands, which he was kissing and pressing to his heart and kissing again and watering with his tears. Everyone shared their tender mood; the women all felt like Mme de la Carlière and the men like the Chevalier. — *That is how the spectacle of virtue works. It gives to a crowd a single thought, a single soul. At such a moment how people respect, how they love, one another! Think of the theater: how beautiful mankind is there, why do they have to separate so soon? Human beings are so good, so happy, when the spectacle of good feeling unites them.* — We were all enjoying this joyous sense of oneness when Mme de la Carlière, on an exalted impulse, rose and said to Desroches: "Chevalier, I do not believe you yet, but soon I shall believe you... — *The little Countess used to do a brilliant imitation of her beautiful cousin in this inspired vein.* — She is better equipped to act it than to feel it.... "Vows pronounced at the foot of the altar," said Mme de la Carlière... You find that funny? — *Forgive me. I can still see the little Countess, hoisted up on the tips of her toes, and hear her solemn tones...* — You are a scoundrel, as corrupt as all the rest of them. I shall tell you no more. — *I promise you not to laugh again.* — Be sure you don't. — *Well then, "Vows pronounced at the foot of the altar..."* — "have so often been followed by betrayals that I attach no weight to tomorrow's promise. We are less frightened by the presence of God than by the opinion of our fellow humans. Monsieur Desroches, come, here is my hand, give me yours and swear me an eternal fidelity and love. Take the people around us as witnesses; agree that if it so turns out that you give me legitimate cause for complaint, I am to denounce you before this tribunal and deliver you over to their indignation; consent to my summoning them and to their calling you traitor, ingrate, deceiver, false and wicked man. They are my friends and yours too; agree that at the moment that I lose you, you lose all of them. And you, my friends; swear to leave him all alone..." At this, the *salon* rang with cries of "I promise," "I permit," "I consent," "We swear ...," and in the midst of this delicious tumult, the Chevalier, who had thrown his arms round Mme de la Carlière, kissed her on the forehead, on her eyes, on her cheeks. "Chevalier!" she cried. "Madame," replied he, "the ceremony is already performed; I am your husband, you are my wife." "In the wild woods, certainly," said she; "but here a trifling little formality is still required. Meanwhile, here is my portrait, do with it what you please. Have you not ordered one of yourself? If so, give me it." Desroches gave a portrait of himself to Mme de la Carlière, who hung it on her arm and, all the rest of the day, insisted that people called her "Madame Desroches." — *I am longing to know what the future held in store.* — You must be patient a moment. I promised you a long story, and I must keep my word. But... yes, it all happened when you were on that long journey and were out of the country.

For two years, two whole years, Desroches and his wife were the most united and happy of couples. Everyone believed that Desroches was quite a new man, and indeed he was. His libertine friends, who had heard about the scene I have described and had been waggish about it, were impressed: they said it showed that all evil luck came from the Priest, and that, after two thousand years, Mme de la Carlière had discovered the secret of escaping the curse of the Sacrament. Desroches had a child by Mme de la Carlière, whom I shall now call "Mme Desroches" until further notice. She absolutely insisted on feeding the child herself. It was a long and dangerous interval for a young man of hot temperament, unused to such a regime. So, while Mme. Desroches was performing her maternal function... — *Her husband went out into society and one day had the misfortune to meet one of those seductive, scheming women, who are angry at the sight of a harmony long banished from their own lives, and who make a hobby and a consolation of plunging others into their own brand of misery.* — That is your story, it is not his. Desroches, who knew himself and who knew his wife and respected and feared her — *It's much the same thing.* — ... passed his days at her side. He was mad about his child, who spent almost as much time in his arms as in its mother's, and, while she was tied by her honorable but tedious duty, he and his friends did their best to keep her amused. — *All very admirable.* — Certainly. One of his friends had been deeply involved in the Government's money-raising schemes, and the Ministry owed him a considerable sum. It represented the bulk of his fortune, but he found it impossible to get them to pay. He discussed it with Desroches, and Desroches remembered he had once been the lover of a woman who had influence in high places and who might be able to help in the affair. He said nothing, but next day he went to see her and have a talk. She was delighted to see, and have the chance of being useful to, this gallant man whom she had loved dearly but had sacrificed to her worldly ambitions. This first meeting was followed by others. The woman was charming; she had been ill-used; and her confiding tone to Desroches was not hard to interpret. Desroches was, for a time, uncertain what to do. — *I can't imagine why.* — But partly from inclination, idleness, or weakness, and partly for fear that a petty scruple — *Over a frolic which could hardly matter to his wife.* — should damp the enthusiasm of his friend's protector and halt her in her efforts, he forgot Mme Desroches for a moment and embarked on an affair, which his accomplice had every reason to keep secret, and on a regular exchange of love letters. They were not able to see each other much, but they wrote very often. I have told lovers a hundred times: "Don't write letters; letters will be your undoing. Sooner or later chance will send one of your letters astray. It is in the nature of chance to contrive every possible circumstance, and it only needs time for it to bring about the fatal one." — *Did none of them believe you.* — No, and all of them were undone, Desroches like a hundred thousand before him and the hundred thousand who will come after. He kept his in one of those little metal-bound caskets. When he was in town or in the country the casket was always under lock and key; on journeys it was put in one of his trunks or stowed in the front of the carriage. This time it was in front. They set off, they arrive. On getting out, Desroches gives his servant the casket to take to his room, which lay beyond his wife's. The clasp breaks, the casket falls to the ground, the lid comes off, and a heap of letters lies at his wife's feet. She picks one or two of them up and sees clear proof of her husband's perfidy. It was a moment that she could never remember afterward without a shudder. She used to tell me that cold sweat broke out on her, all over her body, and it was as if an iron claw was squeezing her heart and compressing her entrails. What was to become of her? What should she do? She composed herself and summoned such reason and strength of mind as remained to her. She selected a few of the most damning of the letters and fitted the lid back on the casket, ordering a servant to place it in his master's room and forbidding him—on pain of dismissal—to reveal what had happened. She had promised Desroches that a complaint would never pass her lips, and she kept her word. Sadness, however, overwhelmed her. She would weep sometimes; she spent her days alone and went for solitary walks; she had her meals brought to her room; she kept up a continuous silence, only broken by a few involuntary sighs. Desroches, distressed at this but unalarmed, treated it as a fit of the vapors, though nursing mothers are not usually subject to the vapors. In a short while, though, his wife's health declined to the point that they had to leave their château and return to town. She persuaded her husband to agree to their traveling separately. Back here in the city she behaved with such discretion and cunning that Desroches, who had not noticed the removal of the letters, looked upon his wife's air of quiet disdain, her indifference, her sighs, her stifled tears and taste for solitude as no more than the normal symptoms of what he imagined to be her illness. Sometimes he advised her not to go on feeding the child herself; but this was in fact her sole means of postponing explanations. Thus Desroches continued to live with his wife in peace of mind, despite her mysterious conduct, till one morning she appeared before him with grand and dignified mien and in the same garb and ornaments as at the domestic ceremony preceding their marriage. What she had lost in freshness and physical beauty, and all that her secret trouble had stolen from her charms, was repaired, and more than repaired, by the nobleness of her demeanor. Desroches was writing to his mistress when his wife entered the room. They were both seized with sudden alarm; but having such a talent, as well as so strong a motive, for concealment, they managed to pass it off. "My dear wife!" exclaimed Desroches at the sight of her, crumpling his letter with pretended casualness meanwhile. "My dear, how lovely you look! What are your plans for today?" "My plan, Monsieur, is for a family gathering. Our friends and relatives have all been invited, and we are counting on you." "But of course. When do you want me?" "When do I want you?... I suppose at the normal time." "I see you have a fan and gloves. Are you going out?" "If you will allow it." "And may I ask where you are going?" "To my mother's." "Please convey my respects to her." "Your respects!" "Certainly." ... Mme Desroches did not return till dinner time. The guests had arrived by then and everyone was waiting. As soon as she appeared, there were the same exclamations as her husband had made; they made a circle round her, men and women alike, exclaiming with one voice: "How beautiful she is today!" The women readjusted a stray curl in her coiffure; the men, standing at a respectful distance and rooted to the spot with awe, kept repeating: "Neither God nor Nature has ever, *could* ever, have made, anything grander, more imposing, more beautiful, more noble, more perfect!" "My dearest wife," said Desroches, "you don't seem to realize the impression you are making. For pity's sake don't smile; a smile, on top of so much beauty, would send us out of our minds." Mme Desroches gave a slight start of annoyance and turned away, raising her handkerchief to her eyes, which had begun to fill with tears. The women, for women notice everything, whispered: "What is the matter with her? She seems almost to be weeping." Desroches, who guessed what they were saying, touched his forehead significantly, signaling that all was not quite right in his wife's head. — *Indeed, so someone wrote to me at the time, there was a rumor that the beautiful Mme Desroches, the beautiful former Mme de la Carlière, had gone mad.* — Dinner was served. Everyone looked in gay mood except Mme de la Carlière. Desroches teased her gently about her solemnity. He and his friends, he told her, would risk their sanity after all, if only she would smile... Mme de la Carlière pretended not to hear and remained grave. The women said that all expressions suited her so well, she should be allowed her choice. The meal ended; they returned to the *salon* and settled in a circle. Mme de la Carlière — *You mean Mme Desroches?* — No, I don't feel like calling her that any longer... Mme de la Carlière rings; she sends for her child. Tremblingly she takes it, uncovers her breast and gives the child suck, then returns it to its nurse, casting a sad look on it and dropping a tear on its face. "It will not be the last," she said, wiping the tear away—words said so softly that they could only be half heard. Everyone was moved by the scene, and a deep silence fell. It was at this moment that Mme de la Carlière rose to her feet and, addressing the assembled company, spoke more or less as follows: "My family, my friends, you were all here on the day that I pledged my troth to M. Desroches and he pledged his to me. No doubt you will remember the conditions upon which I accepted his hand and gave him mine. M. Desroches, tell me, have I kept my vows faithfully?" "To the letter." "Yet you, Monsieur, have deceived me, have betrayed me." "I, Madame?" "You, Monsieur." "Who are the miserable, contemptible...?" "There is only one miserable person, myself, and one contemptible one, you." "Madame... my dear wife..." "I am that no longer." "Madame..." "Monsieur, do not add lies to your arrogance and perfidy. The more you defend yourself, the more confused you will become, so spare yourself." With these words she took the letters from her pocket, gave some to Desroches, and distributed the rest among the company. They took them but made no attempt to read them. "Messieurs, Mesdames," said Mme de la Carlière, "read and judge between us. You shall not leave till you have given your verdict." Then, addressing Desroches: "Monsieur, you will recognize the hand." They all still hesitated, but on her insistence, they read the letters. Desroches, meanwhile, trembling and motionless, leaned his head against a mirror, with his back turned to the company whom he dared not face. One of his friends took pity on him and led him by the hand out of the room. — *According to the accounts I heard, he looked very shabby and mean, and his wife quite magnificently absurd.* — With Desroches out of the room everyone breathed more freely. They all agreed he was at fault and supported Mme de la Carlière in her indignation—so long as she did not take it too far. They clustered round her, arguing and pleading, while the friend who had taken Desroches away went in and out, reporting to him how things were going. Mme de la Carlière remained firm in a resolution that she had not so far made plain. To everything that was said, she had a single answer. To the women it was, "I do not blame you for your indulgence," and to the men, "Messieurs, it cannot be. All trust has gone, and there is no remedy." They brought her husband back, more dead than alive. He fell, rather than threw himself, at his wife's feet and lay there silent. Mme de la Carlière said to him: "Monsieur, get up." He did so; whereupon she added: "You are a bad husband. Are you, or are you not, at least a man of honor? That is what I want to know. I cannot love you or respect you, which is as much as to say that we are not made to live together. I will give up my fortune to you; I only ask enough to keep myself and my child in modest decency. My mother knows my mind; there is a lodging prepared for me in her house, and you must allow me to move there at once. The only favor I ask, and I have the right to ask it, is for you to spare me any public commotion, for it will not shake my resolve and will merely serve to hasten the execution of your cruel sentence upon me. Allow me to take my child with me and to stay by my mother's side till she shall close my eyes for me or I close hers. If this prospect distresses you, be sure that, given my grief and my mother's great age, it will all soon be over..." As she spoke, tears stood in every eye; the women held her hands, the men stood with bowed head. But it was when Mme de la Carlière moved toward the door, with her child in her arms, that the air became full of sobs and cries. Her husband cried: "My wife! My wife! Listen to me. You don't know..." The men and women cried, "Madame Desroches! Madame!" Her husband cried, "My friends, do you mean to let her go? Stop her, stop her for heaven's sake! She must listen to me, I must speak to her..." They urged him to throw himself in her path, but he said, "No, I couldn't, I would not dare. To lay a hand on her! To touch her! I am not worthy..." Mme de la Carlière left. I was at her mother's house when she arrived there, quite broken by all the day's efforts. Three of her servants helped her out of her carriage and carried her in; the nurse followed, as pale as death, with the child asleep in her arms. They laid the unhappy woman on a daybed, where she lay for a long while motionless, watched by her old and worthy mother, who, making noiseless motions with her lips, busied herself around her daughter, wanting to help but not knowing how. At last she regained consciousness. On opening her eyes, her first words where: "So I am not dead? It would be so sweet to be dead. Mother, lie down beside me here and let us both die.... But if we die, who will take care of the child?" At this, she took her mother's dry and trembling hands into one of hers and placed the other on the child. She burst into a flood of tears and struggled to speak, but her words and her sobs were interrupted by a violent hiccup. When at last she could utter, she said, "If only I thought he suffered as much as me!"

In the meantime they tried to console Desroches, attempting to persuade him that his wife's resentment, at a crime so trivial, could not possibly last. She was a proud and sensitive woman and she had been wounded; it was right to allow her a few moments of righteous anger. The solemnity of that extraordinary ceremony of hers made it almost a point of honor for her to take some violent step. "It is just a little bit our fault," said the men. "Yes, very true," said the women. "If we had only seen that sublime mummery in the light that the public and the little Countess did, all this terrible misery would never have happened.... Things done with a certain ritual have a way of catching the imagination, and we stupidly let ourselves be impressed, when we ought to shrug our shoulders and laugh.... You will see, make no mistake, what a laughingstock people will make of this last scene, and the wicked things they will say about us all.... Between ourselves, we were asking for it..."

From this day forward Mme de la Carlière resumed her widowed name and would not allow herself to be called Madame Desroches. Her door, closed for a long time to the world in general, remained closed forever to her husband. He wrote to her, and the letters got burnt unopened. Mme de la Carlière told her family and friends that she would cut off all relations with any who tried to intercede for her husband. The priests did their best to interfere, without success; as for the great ones of this world, she rejected their efforts at peacemaking so crushingly that they soon gave up. — *No doubt they set her down as a pretentious idiot, a self-important prude.* — And others would agree. Meanwhile she was plunged in melancholy; her health declined with extraordinary speed. So many people shared the secret of that unexpected separation and the strange motive behind it that it soon became the talk of the town. This is the moment at which I want you, if you will, to turn your attention away from Mme de la Carlière and toward the Public—that imbecile mob which passes judgment, gives or withholds honor, and raises us to the skies or drags us through the gutter, and which people respect exactly in proportion to their lack of energy and virtue. Slaves of the Public, you may be the tyrant's own adopted son,[2] but do not expect to reign for more than three days! There was but one opinion among the public on Mme de la Carlière's conduct: she was a madwoman and deserved to be locked up. "What an example to give, and to follow! Why at that rate, three-fourths of all married couples would have to part." "Three-fourths, do you say? Are there two in a hundred who are faithful to the letter?... Mme de la Carlière is a lovable woman, no question of that; and she had laid down her conditions, all well and good. Moreover she was beauty, virtue, and high-mindedness in person; and the Chevalier owed her everything. All the same, to demand to be the one woman in the whole kingdom whose husband remains strictly faithful—it is quite too absurd." "And then," so the talk went on, "considering how terribly Desroches is suffering, why does he not go to the law and have that woman brought to reason?" You can judge from this what they would have said, had Desroches or his friend been able to enter into explanations. But everything conspired to keep them silent. All this advice to him, anyway, was the last thing he needed to hear; he would have used any means whatever, apart from force, to win his wife back.

However, Mme de la Carlière was a woman greatly respected, and amid all those carping voices there were one or two which ventured a word in her defense: a very timid, feeble, cautious word, though, said less out of conviction than for the look of the thing. — *In equivocal situations like this, the "respectable" camp always gets swollen by deserters.* — A very true remark. — *Lasting misfortune reconciles, and when a woman loses her good looks the rest of womankind look kindly on her.* — Even truer. And in fact, as the beautiful Mme de la Carlière became the mere specter of her old self, blame of her began to be mitigated by sympathy and commiseration. "To be extinguished in the flower of her age, to perish in such a manner, and by the perfidy of a man whom she had clearly warned, who must have known her character, and who had only the one way of repaying all she had done for him. For, between ourselves, when Desroches married her, he was a younger son from Brittany with nothing to bless himself with but a cloak and a sword... Poor Mme de Carlière! It is really very sad... But still, why not go back to him?... Ah, why? The truth is, everyone has their own character, and it might be better if her kind were more common; it would make our lords and masters think twice."

While these pros and cons were aired over the embroidery frame and the knitting, and while the balance was imperceptibly shifting in Mme de la Carlière's favor, Desroches had fallen into a deplorable condition, both in body and in mind. But he was not to be seen; he had retired to the country, where he waited, in misery and boredom, for some impulse of pity, struggling in vain to obtain it by every kind of submission. For her part Mme de la Carlière, reduced to the last extremity of weakness and exhaustion, found she had to employ a wet nurse to feed her child. The result of the change of milk was just what she had feared; from day to day the child wasted away and at last it died. The talk then ran: "Did you hear? Poor Mme de la Carlière has lost her baby. She must be inconsolable." "Inconsolable? It is even worse. You can't imagine such grief. I have been to see her; it is enough to make you weep, it's unbearable." "And what about Desroches?" "Don't speak to me about men; they are tigers. If that woman meant anything to him, would he still be idling about in the country; would he not have come hurrying back and have waylaid her in the street, or in church, or at her own front door? One can have a door opened to one if one really wants it, by just staying there, sleeping there, dying there..." And the truth is, Desroches had done all of those things, and nobody knew; for the important thing is not knowing but talking. The refrain now became: "The child is dead; but who knows, maybe it would have been a monster like its father?" "The mother is dying; what is her husband doing?" "A good question! He spends the day with his hounds, careering about the forest; and the nighttime he spends swilling with creatures of his own kidney." — *Very natural.* — Then, however, there was a new turn in events. Desroches had risen high in the service, but upon his marriage Mme de la Carlière had made him resign and pass on his regiment to a younger brother. — *Did Desroches have a younger brother?* — No, but Mme de la Carlière had. — *And so?* — And so the young man is killed at his first battle, and now the cry is: "Desroches and evil fortune entered that family hand in hand." To listen to them, one would suppose it was Desroches himself who had given the blow that killed him. It provoked an unleashing of madness on a scale you can hardly conceive. As Mme de la Carlière's troubles mounted, so Desroches' reputation grew blacker; the depth of his betrayal was exaggerated, and, though no more and no less guilty on its account than before, he received more and more odium every day. And do you suppose that was all? No, no. Mme de la Carlière's mother was seventy-six years old. I imagine the death of her grandson and the continued spectacle of her daughter's distress might have helped to shorten her days; still, she was decrepit and infirm. Was this remembered? Not at all. Desroches was responsible for her death too. In fact, not to mince matters, he was a quite abominable wretch whom Mme de la Carlière could have nothing to do with without relinquishing all shame: the murderer of her mother, of her brother, of her son! — *According to that charming logic, if Mme de la Carlière had died—especially after a long and painful illness, so that injustice and public ill will could develop to the full—they ought to have regarded him as the execrable assassin of a whole family.* — That is exactly what happened and what they did. — *Oh, excellent!* — If you do not believe me, ask some of the people here and see what they say. If he stayed on alone in the drawing room today it was because, when he came in, everyone had turned their back on him. — *Why did they do that? One may know a man is a scoundrel, but it doesn't mean one cannot bid him good day.* — The whole affair is still rather recent, and all these people are relations or friends of the deceased. Mme de la Carlière died this year on the day of the second feast of Pentecost; and do you know where? At

St. Eustache, during morning mass, in the middle of a large congregation. — *How ridiculous! One ought to die in one's bed. Whoever thought of dying in church? That woman was determined to be bizarre, right to the end.* — Yes, "bizarre" is the word. She was feeling a little better; she had gone to confession the night before; she thought she was strong enough to go to church to receive the Sacrament instead of having it brought to her home. She is taken to church in a sedan chair. She listens to the office calmly and apparently in no pain. The moment of communion arrives; her women friends take her arm and lead her to the holy table. The priest gives her the wafer; she bows her head as if in thought, and expires. — *She expires!* — Yes, expires—bizarrely, as you said. — *Good God, it must have caused some excitement!* — Let us forget that, you can imagine it; let us get on to what followed. — *Which was that that woman became a hundred times more interesting even than before, and her husband a hundred times more abominable.* — Naturally. — *And that was not all?* — No. As chance would have it, Desroches was in the street as they passed with Mme de la Carlière's body on the way back from the church. — *Everything seems to conspire against that poor devil.* — He comes up, he recognizes his wife, he groans. People inquire who this man is. From the middle of the crowd a reckless voice (the parish priest's) shouts: "He is this woman's assassin!" Desroches, writhing and tearing his hair, cries: "Yes I am, I am..." On the instant the crowd surrounds him, curses him, and picks up stones. He would have been killed on the spot if some decent citizens had not rescued him from the angry mob. — *How had he behaved before, during his wife's illness?* — As well as might be. He was deceived, as we all were, by Mme de la Carlière; she hid her approaching end from others, and perhaps even from herself. — *Yes, and for all that, he was "a barbarous villain, a monster"?* — A raging beast who had driven his sword, inch by inch, into the breast of his saint-like wife, his spouse and benefactress, and had left her to perish without a sign of concern or feeling. — *All through not having known what she was preventing him from knowing?* — And was not known even by the people round her. — *And who saw her every day.* — Precisely; and there you see what it is like, the public's judgment on our private actions. You see how a venial fault... — *Yes, very venial* — is aggravated in its eyes by a sequence of happenings quite impossible to foresee or to prevent. — *And even by circumstances with nothing whatever to do with it originally, like the death of Mme de la Carlière's brother and Desroches' giving up his regiment.* — The truth is, in good matters as in bad, one moment they are absurd panegyrists, the next ridiculous censors. Their only criterion for praise or blame is sheer brute event. My friend, listen to them if you are curious, but do not believe them, and never repeat what they say, for fear of bolstering their absurdity by yours.... But what is on your mind? You seem to be in a dream. — *I am rewriting the plot, imagining Mme de la Carlière acting more normally. She finds the letters; she broods. After some days her resentment brings on an explanation, and the pillow produces a reconciliation, as it so often does. Then, despite all the excuses and protestations and new solemn vows, Desroches' light character leads him into a second lapse; more sulking; another explanation, another reconciliation, further vows, further breakings of vows, and so on for thirty years, in the customary fashion. Desroches, nevertheless, is a decent fellow and he does his best to repair a fairly minor crime by considerateness and thoughtfulness and endless amiability.* — As is not always so customary. — *No separation, no public scenes; they live together as the rest of us do; and the mother-in-law, and the mother, and the brother, and the child die, and no one says a word about it.* — Or if they do, merely to sympathize with an unlucky man, whom fate seems to pursue and overwhelm with misfortunes. — *True.* — From which I conclude that you are not far from granting that stupid monster, with its hundred bad heads and as many bad tongues, all the contempt it deserves. But sooner or later common sense returns, and the wisdom of the future corrects the prattle of the present. — *So you a believe a moment will come when the thing will be seen as it really is and Mme de la Carlière be accused and Desroches absolved?* — I even think the moment is not far off. First of all because the absent are always in the wrong, and no one is more absent than the dead. Secondly because people go on talking and disputing, and the stalest stories are rehashed, and at last they are judged more fairly. For another ten years we may see that poor Desroches, as you have seen him, dragging his miserable existence from one household to another; but eventually people will not shun him so completely, they will question him, they will hear what he has to say, and he will have no reason to keep silent any longer. The facts of his story will become known, and people will begin to call his original folly a mere nothing... — *As it was* — and we are both still young enough to hear the beautiful, the noble, the virtuous, the dignified Mme de la Carlière called a stiff-necked and overweening prude. For people egg one another on and, as they judge without standards, so they speak without measure. — *All the same, if you had a daughter of marrying age, would you give her to Desroches?* — Without hesitation. Because it was chance that first set his foot on those slippery slopes—from which neither you, nor I, nor anyone could have been sure to rescue ourselves; because it was friendship, noble views, and beneficence, as well as a whole crowd of accidents, which led to his fault and help excuse it; because his conduct after his voluntary separation from his wife was beyond reproach; and because, though not approving of unfaithful husbands, I also don't approve of women who attach such importance to that very rare quality, fidelity. And then I have my own ideas, which may be correct but are certainly eccentric, on certain actions which I regard less as vices in mankind than as the consequences of our absurd laws—themselves the source of equally absurd ethical conventions and of what I would like to call an *artificial* depravity.

I am not making myself very clear, but perhaps I could do better another time. Let us go back. I already hear the hoarse voices of ancient she-gamblers summoning you to cards—not to mention that day is closing and night is advancing, with that grand cortege of stars that I promised you. — *Very true.*

SUPPLEMENT TO BOUGAINVILLE'S *VOYAGE*

or

Dialogue between A. *and* B.
On the Inconvenience of Attaching Moral Ideas to Certain Physical Actions Which Do Not Admit of Them

At quanto meliora monet, pugnantiaque istis,
Dives opis Natura suae, tu si modo recte
Dispensare velis, ac non fugienda petendis
Immiscere! Tuo vitio rerumne labores
Nil referre putas?[1]

Hotat, *Sat.* lib. I, *sat.* II, 73 et seq.

· I ·
Judgment on Bougainville's *Voyage*

A. That superb starry vault, under which we came home yesterday and which foretold a fine day, has not kept its promise.
B. You would say so, would you?
A. The fog is so thick we cannot even see the trees.
B. True; but what if this fog, which hangs so low in the atmosphere, being full of moisture, should turn into rain?
A. Or what if, on the contrary, it should rise from these spongy depths and escape to the upper regions, where the air is less dense and may not be, as our chemists call it, "saturated"?
B. We shall have to wait and see.
A. Meanwhile, what are you doing?
B. I am reading.

A. Still that *Voyage* of Bougainville's?
B. Yes.
A. I really don't understand that man. He devotes his youth to mathematics, a sedentary occupation, and then suddenly exchanges meditation and seclusion for the active, grueling, wandering, and footloose life of an explorer.
B. There is no real mystery. A vessel is merely a floating house; and if you think of the navigator, who crosses those vast expanses cooped up in a narrow confine, you might say he was touring the globe on a plank, as we tour the universe on our study floor.
A. There's another seeming oddity, the contradiction between the character of the man and his undertaking. Bougainville has a taste for worldly amusements; he enjoys women, the theater, fine food; he braves the whirlpool of society with as good grace as he does the buffeting waves of ocean. He is amiable and gay; he is a true Frenchman, ballasted on one side by a treatise on the calculus and on the other by a voyage around the globe.
B. He is like everyone else. He likes some amusement after working and to go back to work after he's had some amusement.
A. What do you think of his *Voyage*?
B. So far as I can judge from only a hasty reading, its virtues can be arranged under three headings: a better knowledge of our ancient domicile and its inhabitants; improved security on the seas, which he has traversed plummet in hand; and more accuracy in our maps. Bougainville set off on his voyage with the right intellectual outlook and the qualities needed for success: philosophy, courage, truthfulness; an eye skilled and swift in the art of observation; caution, patience; the desire to see, to understand, to learn; a grasp of calculation, mechanics, geometry, and astronomy, and a sufficient smattering of natural history.
A. And what do you think of his style?
B. Unpretentious, matter-of-fact, simple, and clear—especially if you are familiar with nautical terms.
A. Was his voyage a long one?

B. I've traced it on this globe. Do you see that line of red dots?

A. Beginning at Nantes?

B. Yes, and running toward the Strait of Magellan, entering the Pacific, snaking its way through the islands of that huge archipelago from the Philippines to New Holland, creeping round Madagascar and the Cape of Good Hope, continuing through the Atlantic up the coast of Africa, and completing its circle at the port of departure.

A. Was there much to endure?

B. Every navigator exposes himself, and agrees to expose himself, to the perils of air, fire, earth, and water. But, having wandered for long months between sea and sky and between death and life; having been buffeted by storms and in peril of death from shipwreck and illness, from thirst and famine; that after all this, the unfortunate victim, with his vessel in ruins and he him self dropping with fatigue and starvation, should fall to the mercy of a brazen monster[2] who refuses, or cruelly delays, the most urgently needed help, that is an example of such stony-heartedness...!

A. A crime richly deserving punishment.

B. It was one of the calamities the voyager had not bargained for.

A. And hardly could have done. One imagines that European powers, when sending officials to represent them overseas, would choose only well-intentioned, benevolent men, men full of humanity and able to sympathize...

B. Much they care about that!

A. There are some strange things, I gather, in this *Voyage* of Bougainville's.

B. Yes, many.

A. He says, doesn't he, that wild animals approach man, and birds come and perch[3] on him, when they do not know the danger of such familiarity?

B. Others have said that before him.

A. How does he explain the presence of certain animals on islands separated, by frightening expanses of sea, from any continent?
B. He does not explain it; he merely reports the fact.
A. Well then, how would you explain it?
B. Who knows the early history of our globe? How many stretches of earth, now isolated, were once joined up![4] The only feature one can at all guess at is the direction of the watery mass which separated them.
A. And how would one do that?
B. From the general form of the severed parts. One day, if you like, we might amuse ourselves by studying it. For the present: do you see that island called "The Lancers"?[5] Anyone who examines its location must wonder who could have placed human beings there, what communication they once could have had with the rest of the species, what will happen to them when they multiply on an area no more than one league across?
A. They will eat and exterminate one another; and from that we can perhaps infer a very ancient, and very natural, cannibal epoch, cannibalism being the result of island life.
B. Or alternatively that they restrict population by some superstitious law; a child is crushed, under the feet of a priestess,[6] while still in the womb.
A. Or men have their throats cut by a priest, or there is recourse to castration...
B. Or the infibulation of women. Which leads us on to so many other cruel but necessary customs, the cause of which is lost in the night of time and torments the brains of philosophers. But one fairly constant law is that, over the centuries, supernatural and divine commandments reinforce their hold by turning themselves into civil law, and civil and legal regulations grow sacrosanct and degenerate into supernatural and divine commandments.
A. It is one of the most baneful of palingenesies.

B. Another strand in the cord that binds us.
A. Wasn't Bougainville in Paraguay at the very moment of the expulsion of the Jesuits?[7]
B. Yes.
A. What does he say about it?
B. Less than he might; but enough to teach us that those cruel Spartans in black jackets treated their Indian slaves as the Lacedaemonians did their helots. They condemned them to ceaseless labor; they lived off their sweat; they denied them any right to property; they kept them in degraded superstition; they demanded extreme reverence from them and walked among them whip in hand, hitting out at men and women, young and old. Had it gone on a century longer it would have been impossible to expel them, or at least would have meant a long war between those monks and the Sovereign, whose authority they had begun to shake off.
A. And those Patagonians[8] about whom Doctor Maty and Condamine of the Académie have made such a to-do?
B. They are fine fellows who come up to you and embrace you, crying "Chaoua": strong and vigorous but no more than five foot five or six in height and enormous only as regards their corpulence, the size of their head, and the thickness of their limbs.

Men having a taste for the marvelous anyway, and loving to exaggerate, how should they give the right proportions to objects, when they feel a need to justify their long journey and the trouble they have put themselves to, to see these sights.
A. And what does he think of the savages?
B. It seems to be his daily defending himself against fierce animals that gives the savage the cruel character that he sometimes displays. He is innocent and gentle wherever nothing disturbs his peace and security. All war stems from rival claims to the same property. Civilized man makes a claim, challenged by another civilized man, to a field of which they possess the two extremities, and this field becomes an object of dispute between them.

A. And a tiger and a savage have rival claims to the possession of a forest, which is the original of all claims and the cause of the most ancient war of all... Did you see the Tahitian whom Bougainville took on board and brought back to our country?
B. Yes I saw him; he was called Aotourou.[9] The very first land they came near, he took to be the voyager's native country: whether because they had misrepresented the length of the journey, or because, being naturally deceived by the brief distance to the point where sky and horizon seemed to join, as seen from his own seashore, he did not realize the true scale of the globe. The practice of holding women in common was so rooted in his mind that he threw himself upon the first European woman he encountered and made vigorous efforts to pay her a Tahitian compliment. He became bored among us. The Tahitian alphabet having neither *b*, nor *c*, nor *d*, nor *f*, nor *g*, nor *q*, nor *x*, nor *y*, nor *z*, he never managed to learn our language, which offered his inflexible organs too many unaccustomed articulations and new sounds. He never ceased to sigh for his native land, and this does not surprise me. Bougainville's voyage is the only one that has ever given me a taste for a country not my own; until reading him, I had thought there was nowhere one was so well off as at home. I believed it was the same for all the earth's inhabitants and was a natural attraction in one's own soil, a matter of the advantages one enjoyed there and could not be so sure to find elsewhere.
A. What! So you don't think the Parisian believes grain grows in the Roman Campagna as it does in the fields of Beauce?
B. To tell the truth, no.... Bougainville sent Aotourou home again, paying for his passage and ensuring his safe return.
A. O Aotourou! How happy you must have been to see your father and mother and brothers and sisters and fellow countrymen again! And what will you tell them about us?
B. Not very much, and they won't believe what he does tell them.
A. Why so little?
B. Because he would have understood very little, and because he

wouldn't find words in his own language for the few things he had some idea of.

A. And why should they not believe him?

B. Because in comparing their customs with ours, they will prefer to take Aotourou for a liar than to believe us so mad.

A. You really think that?

B. I have no doubt of it. Savage life is so simple, and our societies are such complicated machines! The Tahitian is close to the origin of the world and the European is close to its old age. The distance which separates him from us is larger than the distance between the newborn child and the decrepit man. He understands nothing about our customs and laws, which appear to him merely shackles, though disguised in a hundred different ways—fetters which can only provoke the indignation and scorn of a being in whom liberty is the profoundest of all feelings.

A. So you subscribe to the "Tahiti fable"?

B. It is not a fable; and you would have no doubts of Bougainville's sincerity if you knew the Supplement to his *Voyage.*

A. And where can I find that?

B. There, on that table.

A. Will you lend it to me?

B. No; but, if you like, we can read it together.

A. I would like to very much. The fog seems to be clearing and blue sky beginning to appear. It seems to be my fate to be in the wrong about the least thing in your eyes. I must have a beautiful nature to forgive you for being so always in the right!

B. Come along, come along; start reading. Skip over the preamble, which tells one nothing, and go straight to the farewell that one of the island chiefs gave to our voyagers. It will give you some notion of those people's eloquence.

A. How did Bougainville come to understand farewells spoken in a language he did not know?

B. You will find out.

• II •
The Old Man's Farewell

It is an old man speaking. He was the father of a large family. On the arrival of the Europeans he looked at them with disdain, though with no sign of astonishment, fear, or curiosity. They approached; and he turned his back on them and returned to his dwelling. His silence and his anxious look revealed his thoughts all too clearly; he was groaning within at the eclipse of all his country's happy days. At Bougainville's departure, when the inhabitants rushed in a crowd to the seashore, clutching his garments, hugging his companions, and weeping, this old man came forward and, with a stern look, said:

"Weep, unhappy Tahitians! Weep—not for the going but for the coming of those wicked and ambitious men. One day you will know them better. There will come a day when they return, in one hand the scrap of wood you see hanging at this man's girdle, in the other the steel you see at that man's side, to bind you in chains, to cut your throats, or enslave you to their whims and vices. One day you will be their servants and as corrupt, as vile, as miserable as them. As for me, I have my consolation: I am near the end of my career, and I shall not see the calamity that I am prophesying. O Tahitians! O my friends! There is a way for you to escape your grim destiny, but I would rather die than teach you. Let them go, let them live."

Then, turning to Bougainville, he added: "And you, you leader of brigands, be quick to take your vessel from our shore. We are innocent, we are happy, and you can only harm our happiness. We follow the pure instinct of nature, and you have tried to erase its trace from our souls. Here, all things belong to all men,[10] and you have preached some strange distinction between *thine* and *mine*. We hold our daughters and wives in common; you have shared this privilege with us and have aroused unknown furies in them. They become mad in your arms, and you become ferocious in theirs. They have begun to hate one another. You cut one another's throats on their behalf, and they return stained with your blood. We are free, and behold, in our very soil you have planted the warrant of our future slavery. You are not a god, neither are you a demon; who are you, then, to make slaves? Orou! You understand these men's language; explain to us, as you did to me, the words written on that strip of metal: *This country belongs to us.*[11] This country yours! Why? Because you set foot in it? If one day a Tahitian were to land on your shores and carve on one of your stones, or the bark of one of your trees, '*This country belongs to Tahiti,*' what would you think? You are the stronger? Well, and what if so? When one of the wretched trifles your boat is full of was stolen, you made an outcry and took revenge; and in the very same moment, in the depths of your heart, you were planning to steal a whole country! You are not slaves, you would suffer death rather than be one, and you want to enslave us! So you believe a Tahitian cannot fight for his liberty and die! The creature you want to seize on, like a brute beast, is your brother. You are both children of nature; what right have you over him that he has not over you? You came here; did we hurl ourselves upon you? Did we pillage your vessel? Did we tie you up and expose you to the arrows of our enemies? Did we yoke you to the plow? We respected our own image in yourselves. Leave us our own customs; they are wiser and more honorable than yours. We have no wish to exchange what you call our ignorance for your useless knowledge. Everything that is good for us, and that we need, we already possess. Are we to be despised for not inventing superfluous needs? When we are hungry, there is food for us; when we are cold, we have stuff to clothe us. You have been inside our huts; what would you say was lacking there? Pursue what you call the conveniences of life as much as you please, but let sensible people cease to do so, when all their painful efforts would bring them is imaginary benefits. If you tempt us beyond the narrow limits of our needs, when will our labor ever end? When shall we enjoy ourselves? We have made the burden of our year's work and our day-to-day labor as light as possible, for rest seems to us the best thing of all. Go back to your own country, and plague and torment yourself there as much as you like, but leave us to our repose. Do not fill our heads with your artificial needs, nor your chimerical virtues. Look at these men. See how upright, healthy, and strong they are. Look at these women; see how healthy, fresh, and beautiful they are. Take that bow. It is mine. Get three or four of your companions to help you bend it. I can bend it unaided. I dig, I climb mountains, I pierce forests, I cover a league of the plain within an hour. Your young men found it hard to keep up with me, and I am over ninety years old. Oh, woeful to this island, woeful to today's Tahitians and to all those to come, was the day you thought to visit us! We only knew one disease, old age, the one that man shares with animals and with plants; but you have given us another. You have infected our blood.[12] We may perhaps have to exterminate, with our own hands, our girls, our women, our children, the men who approached your women and the women who approached your men. Either our fields must welter with the tainted blood which passed from your veins to ours, or our children be doomed to foster the ill you gave to their fathers and mothers, transmitting it age after age to their descendants. Wretch! You will be to blame, either for the ravage of your men's fatal kisses or for the murders we commit to stay the spread of its poison. You speak of crimes! Can you imagine a greater crime than yours? What is the punishment in your country for a man who kills his neighbor? Death by the ax. What is the punishment in your country for the cowardly poisoner? Burning at the stake. Compare your crime with theirs, and tell us, you poisoner of whole nations, what penalty it deserves. Only a short while past the Tahitian girl abandoned herself with rapture to the young Tahitian's embraces; she was all impatience, being now of marrying age, for her mother to lift her veil and uncover her bosom. It made her proud to excite desire, to provoke passionate glances from strangers, from her family, from her own brother. She accepted without shame, before our eyes and among a circle of innocent Tahitians, amid dances and to the sound of flutes, the caresses of him whom her young heart and the secret voice of her senses proclaimed as her own. The idea of crime and the danger of disease entered among us with yourself. Our enjoyments, once so sweet, now come accompanied by remorse and fear. That man in black, who stands beside you listening, spoke to our boys; he said something, I do not know what, to our girls; and now our boys are hesitant, our girls blush. Go and hide yourself, if that is what you wish, in the dark forest with the perverse companion of your pleasures, but allow the good and simple Tahitians to reproduce without shame, in the sight of heaven and broad day. What grander and more honorable sentiment could you find than the one we have taught them and that animates their breast? They believe the moment has come to enrich the nation and the family with a new citizen, and it makes them proud. They eat to live and to grow; they grow in order to multiply; and they find in this neither vice nor shame. Let me list all your misdeeds toward them. You had but to appear among them, and they became thieves. You had but to set foot on our soil, and it ran with blood. That Tahitian who ran to meet you, crying *Taioi*! Friend, friend!—you killed him. And why did you kill him? Because he had been seduced by the glitter of your little serpents' eggs. He gave you fruit; he offered you his wife and daughter; he made you free of his hut; and you slew him for a handful of those beads that he had taken without permission. And the people! At the sound of your murdering arms terror seized them and they fled to the mountains. But do not fancy they would not have returned; had it not been for me, let me tell you, you would all have perished. Ah! Why did I pacify them? Why did I restrain them? Why do I still restrain them now? I do not know; for you deserve no shred of pity, having a savage soul which never once felt pity itself. You and yours have walked our island in peace. You have been respected; all has been yours to enjoy; you have met with no barrier, nor refusal; you were invited in, you were made to sit down, you had the whole riches of the country offered to you. Were you to want young girls? Save those not yet privileged to show their face and bosom unveiled, their mothers gave them to you naked. They were yours, the tender victims of hospitality and its laws. For you and for them the earth was strewn with leaves and flowers; musicians attuned their instruments; nothing troubled the sweetness or disturbed the liberty of your caresses and of theirs. A hymn was sung, exhorting you to be a man and our child to be a woman, a compliant and voluptuous woman. Dances were danced around your couch. And it was fresh from that woman's arms, it was drunk with such sweet raptures on her breast, that you killed her brother, her friend, even perhaps her father. You did even worse. Look there, see that enclosure bristling with arrows; see those arms, till now only used against our enemies, turned against our own children. See the unhappy companions of your pleasures; see their sadness; see their fathers' sorrow and their mothers' despair; it is there that they must perish, either by our hand, or by the sickness that you have given them. Begone from here, unless your cruel eyes relish the spectacle of death; go, begone, and may the guilty seas which brought you here unscathed purge their fault and give us revenge by engulfing you ere you return. And you, Tahitians, return to your huts, return I say; and let these unworthy strangers, as they depart, hear only the cry of the sea and behold only the sea's foam whitening a deserted shore."

Scarcely had he done, when the crowd of inhabitants disappeared. A vast silence reigned over the whole isle, and the only sound to be heard was the shrill whistling of the wind and the quiet murmur of waters along all the length of the coast. It was as if the air and the sea, hearing the old man's voice, had it in mind to obey him.

B. Well, what do you think of it?
A. It is a violent speech all right; but behind the abruptness and the savage accent I seem to detect European ideas and European turns of phrase.
B. You need to remember that it is a translation from Tahitian into Spanish and from Spanish into French. The night before, the old man had gone to see Orou, whose family had kept up the use of Spanish for generations. Orou had questioned him and written out his harangue in Spanish, and Bougainville had a copy of this in his hand while the old man was speaking.
A. I see all too well now why Bougainville suppressed this fragment. But it seems not to be all, and I feel no small curiosity about the rest.
B. It may perhaps not interest you so much.
A. That doesn't matter.
B. It is a conversation between the ship's chaplain and one of the island's inhabitants.
A. Orou?
B. Yes. When Bougainville's vessel approached Tahiti, a vast swarm of dugouts took to the sea. In an instant his ship was surrounded with them; wherever he looked, he saw demonstrations of surprise and benevolence. They threw him provisions; they clambered up the ropes and clung to the ship's sides; they crowded on to his gig, exchanging shouts with those on shore, and the whole population of the island rushed to the scene. Soon the whole crew was on the beach. The islanders separated them, each taking one of them to his own hut, the men hugging them warmly round their waists, the women stroking their cheeks. Put yourself in their position; be a witness, in thought, to this scene of hospitality, and tell me what feeling it gives you about the human species.
A. A very beautiful one.
B. But while I remember, I ought to tell you about a rather strange event. That scene of benevolence and humaneness was suddenly

disturbed by the cries of a man calling for help. It was the servant of one of Bougainville's officers. Some young Tahitians had thrown themselves on him, stretching him on the ground, and were stripping him and preparing to do him a "courtesy."

A. What, those simple, innocent people, those good, decent savages...?

B. You have not understood. The servant was a woman disguised as a man.[13] None of the crew had discovered it, throughout the voyage, but the Tahitians realized her sex at the first glance. She was born in Burgundy and was called Barre. She was twenty-six and not exactly ugly or exactly pretty. She had never left her village, but her chosen notion of a journey was to go round the globe; she was, always, a thoroughly sensible and brave young woman.

A. Those frail organisms sometimes harbor mighty souls.

· III ·
The Chaplain's Conversation with Orou

B. In the sharing-out of Bougainville's crew, the Chaplain[14] fell to Orou. They were about the same age, thirty-five or thirty-six. Orou at this time had a wife and three daughters, called Asto, Palli, and Thia. They undressed the Chaplain, washed his face, hands, and feet, and served him a wholesome and frugal meal. As he was about to go to bed, Orou, who had gone off with his family, reappeared and presented his wife and his three naked children, saying: "You have had supper, you are young, you are in good health; if you sleep alone, you will sleep badly, a man needs a companion at his side at night. Here is my wife, here are my daughters: choose the one who suits you, but if you wish to oblige me, you will give the preference to the youngest of my daughters, who has not yet had any children."

The mother added: "Alas, it is not for me to complain. Poor Thia! It is not her fault."

The Chaplain replied that his religion, his calling, and sheer decency and good morals forbade him to accept these offers.

Orou replied: "I do not know what this thing is that you call 'religion,'[15] but I cannot believe it is good, since it prevents you from enjoying an innocent pleasure, one to which nature, our sovereign mistress, invites us all; since it prevents you from giving existence to a fellow mortal, from doing a service asked of you by a father, a mother, and their children, from repaying a host who has given you a warm welcome, and from enriching a nation by endowing it with another citizen. I do not know what kind of thing a 'calling' is, but your first duty is to be a man and to show gratitude. I, Orou, your host and your friend, do not ask you to carry my customs back to your own country; but I beg you to fall in with them here. Are the customs of Tahiti better or worse than yours? There is an easy answer to that: does the country where you were born have more men than it can feed? In that case your customs are neither worse nor better than ours. Could it feed more than it has? Then our customs are better than yours. As to the matter of decency that you mentioned, I understand, I see I was wrong and I beg your pardon. I do not wish you to injure your health; if you are tired, then you must sleep. Only I hope you will not always sadden us in this way. See the look of concern on those faces: they are afraid you have seen some defect in them which makes you despise them. But even were it so, would it not be pleasure enough for you to honor one of my daughters among her companions and sisters and so perform a good deed? Be generous!"

THE CHAPLAIN

It's not that. They are all equally beautiful. But think of my religion! Think of my calling!

OROU

They belong to me, and I am offering them to you. They belong to themselves, and they give themselves to you. However pure a conscience the thing named *religion* and the thing named a *calling* demand, you can accept them without scruple. It is no abuse of authority on my part; I assure you I know and I respect the rights of individuals.

Here the honest Chaplain has to admit, Providence had never exposed him to such a pressing temptation. He was young; he was in a fever; he tore his gaze away from the amiable suppliants, he let it be drawn back to them; he lifted his eyes and his hands to heaven. Thia, the youngest, clasped his knees and said: "Stranger, do not distress my father, do not distress my mother, do not distress me! Do me honor in the hut and among my own people; raise me to the rank of my sisters, who make fun of me. Asto, the eldest, already has three children; Palli, the second, has two; and Thia has none! Stranger, worthy stranger, do not rebuff me! Make me a mother. Give me a child whom, one day, I can walk with hand in hand; a child all may see at my bosom in nine months' time; an object of pride and a part of my dowry when I pass from my father's hut to another's. I shall perhaps be more lucky with you than with our young Tahitians. If you grant me this favor, I shall never forget you; I shall bless you all my life; I shall write your name on my arm and on your son's; we will always repeat your name with joy, and when you quit these shores, my wishes will pursue you across the seas till you are safely home."

The ingenuous Chaplain says that she clasped his hands and gave him such touching and expressive looks; that she wept; that her father, her mother, and her sisters left the scene; that, left alone with her and still repeating "My religion! My calling!" he woke next morning to find himself beside this young woman, who was covering him with caresses and invited her father, her mother, and her sisters, when they came to the bedside, to add their thanks to hers.

Asto and Palli went away and returned with meats of the country and fruit and wine. They embraced their sister and wished her happiness. The party all breakfasted together, after which

Orou, being left alone with the Chaplain, said to him: "I can see that you have made my daughter happy, and I thank you. But could you explain to me that word *religion,* which you have so often pronounced and with such sadness?"

The Chaplain, after a moment's meditation, replied: "Who made your hut and the utensils in it?"

OROU

I did.

THE CHAPLAIN

Well, we believe that this world and all it contains is the work of a workman.

OROU

Does he have feet, hands, and a head?

THE CHAPLAIN

No.

OROU

Where does he live?

THE CHAPLAIN

Everywhere.

OROU

Even here!

THE CHAPLAIN

Even here.

OROU

We have never seen him.

THE CHAPLAIN

One cannot see him.

OROU

He does not seem much of a father. But I suppose he must be rather old. He must be at least as old as his creation.

THE CHAPLAIN

He does not age. He spoke to our ancestors; he gave them laws; he told them how he wished to be honored; he commanded them to perform certain actions, as being good, and forbade them to commit others, as being bad.

OROU

I see; and one of the actions he forbade was to sleep with a woman or a girl? If so, why did he create two sexes?

THE CHAPLAIN

So that they might unite; but on certain specified conditions and after certain preliminary ceremonies, after which a man belongs to a woman and belongs only to her, and a woman belongs to a man and only to him.

OROU

For their whole life?

THE CHAPLAIN

For their whole life.

OROU

So that if a wife happens to sleep with another man, or a husband to sleep with another woman... but that will not happen, since, he being there, and such a thing being displeasing to him, he can prevent it.

THE CHAPLAIN

No, he lets them do as they will, and if they do it they sin against the law of God (for that is the name we give to the great workman) and against the law of the country, and they commit a crime.

OROU

I would hate to offend you. But if you would allow me, I could give you my own opinion.

THE CHAPLAIN

Do so.

OROU

I find those strange commands you mention opposed to nature and contrary to reason; they seem to me designed to multiply crimes and produce continual annoyance for the old workman—the one who made everything without the aid of a head or hands or tools, who is everywhere and is not to be seen anywhere, who exists today, exists tomorrow, and is never a day older, who commands and is not obeyed, who could prevent things and does not. I find them contrary to nature because they imply that a feeling, thinking, and free being can be the property of another being of the same kind. What could be the grounds for such a right? Do you not see that in your country you have made a confusion between things which have neither feeling, nor thought, nor desire, nor will and can be given or taken, kept or exchanged, without suffering or complaint, and things which *cannot* be exchanged or owned, things which have liberty and will and desire, can give or withhold themselves for a moment or forever, things which complain and suffer and can never be made items of commerce without forgetting their character or doing violence to their nature. I find these commands contrary to the general law of beings. Does anything, really, seem more senseless than a commandment which makes a sin of the changeableness which is in all of us and dictates a constancy which is not to be found in any of us, which violates the nature and the liberty of man and woman by chaining them to each other forever? Could anything seem more mad than a fidelity which confines the most capricious of enjoyments to a single individual? than a vow of immutability by two creatures of flesh and blood, in the sight of a heaven never two instants the same, beneath caverns which menace ruin, under a rock crumbling into dust, at the foot of a tottering tree and standing upon shifting stone? Believe me, you have brought mankind to a plight worse than the animals'. I know nothing of your great workman, but I am glad he did not speak to our fathers, and I hope he will not speak to our children, for he might by chance tell them the same stupidities, and they might perhaps be stupid enough to believe them. Yesterday at supper you talked to us about magistrates and priests. I do not know what sort of thing they are, these *magistrates* and *priests* whose authority regulates your conduct, but tell me, are they the masters of good and evil? Can they make just things unjust and unjust things just? Have they the power to attach goodness to harmful actions and evil to innocent and useful ones? You can hardly believe so, for, on that basis, there would be neither true nor false, neither good nor bad, neither beautiful nor ugly—or at least only what it pleases your great workman, your magistrates, and your priests to pronounce as such, and from moment to moment you would have to change your ideas and your conduct. One day, by one or other of your three masters, you would be given the command *kill,* and you would be obliged, in conscience, to kill; another day, *steal,* and you would be expected to steal; or, *do not eat that fruit,* and you would not dare to eat it; or *I forbid you that vegetable, or that animal,* and you would take care not to touch it. There is no sort of goodness that might not be forbidden you, or wickedness you might not be ordered to do. And where will you be if, your three masters being apt to disagree, one of them decides to permit, one to command, and one to forbid you to do the same thing, as I imagine often happens? Then, to please the priest you will have to quarrel with the magistrate, to satisfy the magistrate you will have to displease the great workman, and to keep on good terms with the great workman you will have to renounce nature. And do you know what the result will be? It means you will despise all three, and you will be neither a man, nor a citizen, nor pious; you will be nothing at all; you will be on bad terms with every kind of authority, on bad terms with yourself, malevolent, tormented by your own heart's feelings, and unhappy, as I saw you last night, when I offered you my daughter and you cried: "Think of my religion, think of my calling!" Do you want to know what is good and what is evil at all times and in all places? Then fix your eye on the nature of things, on your relationship with your fellow-men, on the influence of your conduct on your private benefit and on the public good. You are mad if you think there is anything in the universe, high or low, which can add to or take away from the laws of nature. Her eternal will is that the good shall be preferred to the bad and the general good to the particular. Command the opposite as much as you wish, you will not be obeyed. You will multiply evildoers and the unhappy by fear, by punishment, and by remorse; you will deprave consciences; you will corrupt minds; people will no longer know what they are supposed to do or avoid doing. Troubled when they are innocent, at peace with themselves in crime, they will have lost sight of their Pole star, their right road.

Tell me honestly: despite the express commands of your three legislators, does not a young man ever sleep with a young woman?

THE CHAPLAIN

It would be a lie if I said so.

OROU

Does a woman who has sworn to belong to none but her husband never give herself to another man?

THE CHAPLAIN

Nothing is more common.

OROU

Either your legislators penalize it severely, or they do not. If they do, they are savage brutes doing violence to nature; if they do not, they are idiots who have exposed their authority to scorn by a useless prohibition.

THE CHAPLAIN

The guilty parties, if they escape legal penalty, are punished by public censure.

OROU

That is to say: justice only comes into its own where common sense fails, and the law has to be helped out by the madness of public opinion.

THE CHAPLAIN

A girl who is disgraced cannot find a husband.

OROU

Disgraced? Why?

THE CHAPLAIN

An unfaithful wife is more or less generally despised.

OROU

Despised? Why?

THE CHAPLAIN

The young man is called a cowardly seducer.

OROU

Cowardly! A seducer! Why?

THE CHAPLAIN

The father, the mother, and the child herself are all grief-stricken. An unfaithful husband is a libertine; a husband who has been betrayed shares in his wife's shame.

OROU

What a monstrous tissue of absurdities you are describing. And you have not told me all: for as soon as one is allowed to apply the ideas of justice and property as one chooses, allowed to give or deny qualities to things arbitrarily, allowed to attribute good and evil and their opposites to actions according to one's fancy, one will begin blaming others, accusing others, suspecting and tyrannizing over others, becoming envious and jealous, deceitful and hurtful, secretive and false; one will spy and lay traps and quarrel and lie. Daughters will deceive their parents, husbands their wives and wives their husbands. Girls—yes, it will come to that—will suffocate their young; suspicious fathers will despise and neglect theirs; and mothers will abandon them to the mercy of fate, and crime and debauchery will flourish in a hundred forms. I know all this, as if I had lived among you. It is so, because it must be so; and society, which your leader so praises for its beautiful "order," will be no more than a collection, either of hypocrites, who secretly trample on the law, or unfortunates, the willing instruments of their own suffering, or imbeciles, in whom prejudice has quite stifled the voice of nature, or mere monsters and freaks in whom nature renounces her rights.

THE CHAPLAIN

It is not an unfair picture. But in your country, do you not marry?

OROU

Yes, we marry.

THE CHAPLAIN

What is marriage, with you?

OROU

Consent to live in the same hut and sleep in the same bed, so long as we are happy in doing so.

THE CHAPLAIN

And when you are not?

OROU

We separate.

THE CHAPLAIN

What becomes of your children?

OROU

O stranger! Your last question finally shows me the depths of your country's misery. Know, my friend, that here the birth of a child is always an occasion for happiness and its death a subject for regret and tears. A child is a precious good, because it must become a man, and we cherish it with a quite different care than we give to our animals and our plants. A newborn infant causes both private and public joy: it is an increase of wealth for the hut and of strength for the nation; it means more arms and hands in

Tahiti; we see in the child a future farmworker, fisherman, hunter, soldier, husband, and father. On returning from her husband's hut to her parents', a wife will bring back with her the children she took there as a dowry. The ones born during their life together are shared out; and we try to keep a balance, giving each partner the same number of girls and boys.

THE CHAPLAIN

But children have to be looked after for many years before they become useful.

OROU

We assign a sixth part of the country's wealth to their support and to the needs of the old. This grant follows them wherever they go. Thus, you see, the bigger a Tahitian family is, the richer it becomes.

THE CHAPLAIN

A sixth part!

OROU

It's a sure way of encouraging population and respect for old age and proper care of children.

THE CHAPLAIN

Do your husbands and wives sometimes reunite?

OROU

Very often. However, the shortest length for a marriage is from one moon to another.

THE CHAPLAIN

Unless the wife is pregnant; and then they must live together for at least nine months?

OROU

No, not so. Paternity, like the child-grant, follows the child everywhere.

THE CHAPLAIN

You mentioned children brought by a wife as a dowry?

OROU

Exactly. Take the case of my eldest daughter. She has three children; they can walk; they are healthy; they promise to be strong. When the fancy takes her to marry again, she will take them with her. They are hers. Her husband will receive them with joy, and she will please him all the more if she is pregnant with a fourth.

THE CHAPLAIN

By him?

OROU

By him, or by some other man. The more children our daughters have, the more they are sought after; the more vigorous and good-looking our sons are, the richer they will be. Also, to the same degree that we carefully protect the one from approaches by men and the other from dealings with women before the age of fecundity, when the boys reach puberty and the girls are marriageable we are urgent with them to reproduce. You cannot imagine what a service you will have done my daughter Thia if you have given her a child. Her mother will not have to say to her at each new moon, "Thia, what can you be thinking of? You are not pregnant. You are nineteen years old; you ought to have had two children already, and you have none. Who is going to take care of you? If you waste the years of your youth like this, what will you do in your old age? Thia, you must have some defect which puts men off. Take yourself in hand my child. At your age, I had been a mother three times."

THE CHAPLAIN

What precautions do you take to protect your adolescent girls and boys?

OROU

That's the leading part of home education and the most important point in public morality. Our boys, up to the age of twenty-two, that is to say two or three years after puberty, wear a long tunic and a little chain round their loins. Our daughters, before marriageable age, would not dare go out without a white veil. To take off one's chain, to raise one's veil, is a crime that only rarely they commit, because from early on we teach them its dangerous consequences. But at the moment when the young male reaches his full strength, when the symptoms of his virility are continuous and the frequency of his emissions and the quality of the seminal fluid give us confidence; at the moment when a young girl begins to droop and languish and is of an age to conceive desires, to provoke them, and to satisfy them effectively; at this moment, a father will remove his son's chain and cut the nail of his right-hand middle finger, and a mother will lift her daughter's veil. The one is allowed to solicit women and be solicited by them, and the other to walk in public with her face uncovered and her bosom bare and accept or refuse a man's caresses. We merely indicate to them in advance which girls the boys, and which boys the girls, would do best to prefer. The emancipation of a girl or a boy is a great celebration. If it is a girl, the young men gather outside her hut the night before and all night the air resounds with song and the sound of instruments. On the day itself, her father and mother lead her to an enclosure where there is dancing and jumping, wrestling and running. They display the man naked before her, so she can see him from all sides and in every posture. Or if it is a young man's day, it is for the girls to do the honors and display the young woman naked to him, without reserve or secrecy. The ceremony is finally completed on a bed of leaves, as you saw when you came among us. At the fall of night the girl may return to her parents' hut or may go to that of her chosen man, where she will stay as long as she feels inclined.

THE CHAPLAIN

So that celebration may be, or may not be, a wedding day?

OROU

Exactly...

A. What's that I see in the margin?
B. It's a note in which the worthy Chaplain says that the parents' precepts on the selection of young men and oung women were full of good sense and acute and useful observations, but that he had suppressed this catechism, since to people as corrupt and superficial as ourselves it would have appeared unpardonably licentious. He adds, however, that it was not without regret that he cut out details in which was to be seen, first of all, just how far a nation, which continually concerned itself with some great purpose, can progress without the aid of physics and anatomy; and secondly, how different are ideas of beauty in a country which relates visual forms to passing pleasures from those of a country which relates them to lasting utility. In the former, to be beautiful, a woman has to have a brilliant complexion, a broad brow, large eyes, fine and delicate features, a slim waist, a small mouth, and little hands and feet.... Here, almost none of these things come into the calculation. The woman who catches our eyes and inflames our desires is the one who (like the wife of Cardinal d'Ossat) gives promise of numerous children—and of active, intelligent, brave, healthy, and robust ones. There is almost nothing in common between the Venus of Athens and the Venus of Tahiti; the one is the Venus of flirtation, the other of fecundity. A Tahitian woman once said scornfully to another, "You are beau-

tiful, but you produce ugly children; I am ugly, but I produce beautiful children. I am the one the men prefer."

After that note of the Chaplain's, Orou's discourse continues.
A. Before it does so, I have a favor to ask. Will you remind me of that New England anecdote?
B. It ran like this. A young woman called Polly Baker,[16] having become pregnant for the fifth time, was summoned before the tribunal of justice of Connecticut, near Boston. The law condemns all persons of her sex who only owe the name of mother to loose behavior to a fine, or to corporal punishment if they cannot pay the fine. Miss Polly, on entering where the magistrates were assembled, addressed them thus: "Sirs, allow me say a few words. I am an unfortunate and penniless girl, without the means to pay a lawyer to defend me, so I shall be brief. I shall not try to argue that the sentence you mean to pass on me is against the law; what I am daring to hope is that you will ask the government, in its charity, to waive the fine. This is the fifth time I have appeared before you on the same charge. Twice I have paid heavy fines, twice I have undergone public and shameful punishment because I was not in a position to pay. This may be in accordance with the law, I do not dispute it: but sometimes there are unjust laws, in which case they get abrogated; and sometimes laws are too severe, and the legislature can waive their execution. I shall be so bold as to say that the one under which I am condemned is both unjust in itself and too severe toward me. I have never injured any of my neighbors, and I defy my enemies, if I have any, to prove I have done the slightest wrong to man, woman, or child. Suppose for a second that the law did not exist: then I cannot see what my crime is. I have brought five beautiful children into the world, at the risk of my life; I have fed them with my own milk; I have supported them with the labor of my hands; and I would have done even more for them if the fines which I had to pay had not put it out of my power. Is it a crime to augment His

Majesty's subjects, in a new country which is in need of inhabitants? I have stolen no woman's husband nor debauched any young man; no one has ever accused me of such things, and if anyone complains of me it will perhaps be the Minister, for not paying him my marriage dues. But is that my fault? I appeal to you, Sirs; you will grant me enough good sense to prefer the honorable status of marriage to the shameful condition I have lived in up to now. I have always wanted, and I still want, to be married, and I will be so bold as to claim that I would have the good conduct, industriousness, and economy proper to a wife, as I already have the fecundity. I defy anyone to say I have refused the married state. I consented to the first, and only, proposal ever made to me. I was still a virgin; I was simple enough to entrust my honor to a man who had none. He gave me my first child and deserted me. You all know that man. He is now a magistrate like yourselves and sits at your side. I was hoping that he would appear here today and would have moved you to take pity on me—on an unfortunate woman who is so only because of him. In that case I could not have brought myself to put him to shame, by recalling what happened between us. Am I wrong to complain, today, of the injustice of the law? The original cause of my errors, my seducer, is raised to power and honors by the same government that punishes my misfortunes with the whip and ignominy. You will say I have transgressed against the commands of religion. But if my offense is against God, leave the punishing of it to him. You have already excluded me from church communion, is that not enough? Why, to the torments of hell, which you believe await me in the next world, do you have to add fines and whipping in this one? You will, Sirs, forgive these reflections of mine. I am not a theologian, but I find it hard to believe it a great crime on my part to have given life to beautiful children, children to whom God has granted immortal souls and who worship him. If you mean to make laws which change the nature of actions and turn them into crimes, make some against bachelors, who grow more plentiful every day and carry seduction and opprobrium into families, deceive young women like myself, and force them to live in my shameful condition. They are the real disturbers of the peace; you have crimes there that deserve the attention of the law more than mine."

This strange speech produced the effect that Miss Baker had hoped for; her judges remitted her fine and the alternative penalty. Her seducer, learning of what had happened, felt remorse at his earlier conduct and wanted to repair it. Two days later he married Miss Baker and made an honest woman of one whom five years before he had forced to become a harlot.

A. And you have not made up that story yourself?

B. No.

A. I am glad.

B. I have a feeling that the abbé Raynal reports the story and Polly's speech in his *History of Trade in the Two Indies.*

A. An excellent work, and written in a tone so different from his previous ones that people have suspected him of calling in helping hands.

B. That is an injustice.

A. Or a piece of malice. The world lays rough hands on the laurels round a great man's head, stripping them to their last leaf.

B. But time gathers up the scattered leaves and weaves him a crown once more.

A. But by that time the man is dead. He will have felt the injury done him by his contemporaries and will be numb to the reparation he wrings from posterity.

· IV ·
Continuation of the Conversation between the Chaplain and the Tahitian

OROU

What a moment of happiness for a young woman and her parents when she proves to be pregnant! She gets up; she rushes and throws her arms round her mother's and father's necks; she announces the news, and they hear it, with transports of joy. "Mama! Papa! Kiss me; I am pregnant." "Do you really mean it?" "I do! I do!" "And who by?" "By so-and-so..."

THE CHAPLAIN

How does she know who the father is?

OROU

Why shouldn't she? Our love affairs are like our marriages, they last a least from one moon to the next.

THE CHAPLAIN

And is that rule strictly observed?

OROU

You will have to judge for yourself. Anyway, the time between two moons is not a long one. But if two fathers have strong claims to the begetting of the same child, it no longer belongs to its mother.

THE CHAPLAIN

Whom does it belong to then?

OROU

To the one she chooses to give it to; that is all the privilege left to her. But, a child being an object of great value in itself, loose women—as you will imagine—will be rare and young men will steer clear of them.

THE CHAPLAIN

So you have loose women too? It is a comfort at least to hear that.

OROU

We have more than one kind, as a matter of fact. But you are making me digress. When one of our daughters becomes pregnant, if the father-to-be is a handsome, well-made, brave, intelligent, and hardworking man, we have an extra cause for happiness, the hope that the child will inherit the father's virtues. The only cause for shame on her part would be to have made a bad choice. You can imagine how much we value health, beauty, energy, industriousness, and courage. You will realize how, in the nature of things, the prerogatives of blood will persist from generation to generation. You who have visited many lands, tell me if in any you have seen so many handsome men, so many beautiful women as in Tahiti! Look at me; what do you think of me? Well, there are ten thousand here taller than me and as robust—though not braver than me; and mothers often point me out to their daughters.

THE CHAPLAIN

But of the children you have fathered outside your own hut, what proportion belong to you?

OROU

Every fourth one, whether a girl or a boy. We have established a circulation of men, women, and children, of able-bodied workers of every age and type of skill; it is ten times better than your own circulation of mere commodities, or the things that workers produce.

THE CHAPLAIN

I can believe it. What are those black veils[17] that I sometimes see?

OROU

The sign of sterility, resulting from some birth defect or from age. A woman who leaves off her veil and mixes with men is a libertine, and a man who lifts her veil and makes approaches to a sterile woman is a libertine.

THE CHAPLAIN

And those gray veils?

OROU

The sign of a woman's monthly sickness. A woman who leaves off this veil and mixes with men is a libertine, and a man who lifts her veil and approaches a woman with her "monthly" is a libertine.

THE CHAPLAIN

Do you have punishments for such cases?

OROU

None apart from public blame.

THE CHAPLAIN

Can a father sleep with his daughter, or a mother with her son, or a brother with his sister, or a husband with another man's wife?

OROU

Why not?

THE CHAPLAIN

One can perhaps overlook fornication; but incest! adultery!

OROU

What do you mean by those words *fornication, incest, adultery*?

THE CHAPLAIN

They are crimes, enormous crimes. For one of them you can be burned in my country.

OROU

Whether they burn you or not in your country bothers me very little. You would not judge European morals by those of Tahiti, so do not judge Tahitian ones by yours. One needs a surer rule; and what shall that rule be? Do you know of a better than the public good and private utility? In the present case: tell me in what way your crime of *incest* goes against these two aims. You are mistaken, my friend, if you believe that, once a law has been passed, a shameful name invented, and a penalty specified, there is nothing more to be said. Tell me, what do you mean by *incest*?

THE CHAPLAIN

Incest! Why...

OROU

Yes, this *incest*...? Is it very long since your great workman, who has no head nor hands nor tools, made the world?

THE CHAPLAIN

No.

OROU

Did he create the whole human species in the same moment?

THE CHAPLAIN

He only created one man and one woman.

OROU

Did they produce children?

THE CHAPLAIN

Certainly.

OROU

Suppose the two original parents only had daughters and the mother died first, or that they only had sons and the wife lost her husband...

THE CHAPLAIN

You are embarrassing me. Whatever you say, *incest* is an abominable crime. Let us change the subject.

OROU

I do not see why. I shall not say another word till you explain what that abominable crime of *incest* is.

THE CHAPLAIN

Very well! I admit that perhaps *incest* does no harm to nature. But isn't it sufficient that it is a threat to the state? Where would be the security of sovereigns, or the safety of society, if a whole nation, several millions of humans, were attached to a mere fifty fathers?

OROU

At worst it would mean that where there might have been one single great society there would be fifty smaller ones, more happiness and one crime the less.

THE CHAPLAIN

I suspect, though, that even in Tahiti a son does not often sleep with his mother.

OROU

No, unless he has peculiar respect for her, and a tenderness which makes him forget the difference in age and prefer a woman of forty to a girl of nineteen.

THE CHAPLAIN

And relationships between fathers and daughters?

OROU

They are hardly more common, except where the daughter is ugly and not much sought after. Then, if her father is fond of her, he will do his best to give her a dowry of children.

THE CHAPLAIN

I have the impression that the fate of women not privileged by nature cannot be a very happy one in Tahiti.

OROU

That shows me you do not have a high opinion of our young men's generosity.

THE CHAPLAIN

As for unions between brothers and sisters, I imagine they are very common.

OROU

And highly approved of.

THE CHAPLAIN

Listening to you, one would believe that this passion, which produces so many crimes and evils in our countries, is altogether innocent here.

OROU

Stranger! You have bad judgment as well as a bad memory. Bad judgment because, wherever there is a prohibition, people are tempted to break it and will do so. Bad memory, because you are forgetting what I told you. We have old reprobates who go out at night without their black veils and receive men, though no fruit can come of it. If they are recognized or taken by surprise, their punishment is exile to the north of the island, or slavery. We have precocious girls, who lift their white veil unbeknown to their parents. There is a locked room for them in the hut. We have young men who take off their chain before the time prescribed by nature and by law, and we reprimand their parents. We have wives who find the time of pregnancy too long for them, and women and girls who are not scrupulous about their gray veil. But on the whole we do not attach great importance to any of these faults. You cannot imagine how the idea of wealth, attached as it is in our minds to the idea of population, purifies our morals on this point.

THE CHAPLAIN

Does the passion of two men for the same woman or the fancy of two women or two girls for the same man not cause disorders?

OROU

I have hardly seen four instances of it. The woman's choice or the man's choice is the end of the matter. If a man became violent, it would be a grave offense; but there would need to be a public complaint against him, and it is practically unheard of for a girl or a woman to complain. The only thing I have noticed is, our women do not show as much pity toward ugly men as our young men do toward ill-favored women; but we do not let it bother us.

THE CHAPLAIN

So far as I can see, you scarcely know what jealousy is; which must mean that marital tenderness and fatherly love, which are such sweet and potent sentiments, must be, if not totally unknown among you, at least barely felt.

OROU

We have filled their place by another sentiment, altogether more universal, energetic, and durable: self-interest. Put your hand on your heart: forget that fanfaronade of virtue always on your comrades' lips and nowhere found in their hearts. Tell me if, in whatever country, there is a father who, were he not restrained by shame, would not willingly lose his child, or a husband who would not willingly lose his wife, rather than lose his fortune or all his worldly comforts. Wherever, on the other hand, man has the same interest in his fellowman's well-being as he has in his own bed, his own health, his repose, his hut, his fields, and his crops, he will do everything possible for his fellowman. It is among such that a child's sickbed is watered with tears; where a mother is nursed tenderly through illness; where a fertile woman, a marriageable girl, an adolescent boy are highly prized and every care is lavished on their upbringing, because their survival is an increase of riches and their loss an impoverishment.

THE CHAPLAIN

I rather fear the savage may be in the right. Our own wretched peasant wears his wife out to spare his precious horse; he leaves his child to perish without aid but calls in the doctor to attend his ox.

OROU

I do not understand all you say; but on your return to that so-called civilized country of yours, try to introduce our system. Then you will really find the value of a newborn child and the importance of population. Shall I explain a secret to you? But be careful not to pass it on. You arrive here. We deliver our wives and daughters up to you. You are astonished; you express your gratitude in a way that makes us laugh; you thank us for imposing the heaviest of all taxes on you and your companions. We did not ask money of you; we did not hurl ourselves on your merchandise, for we despised your goods; but our wives and daughters came and filched the blood from your veins. When you go, you will have left children behind; this tax on your person, on your very substance, is worth more than all the rest, wouldn't you agree? And if you want to know its value, imagine you have two hundred leagues of coast to traverse, and every twenty miles you pay the same sort of levy. We have vast tracts of land lying idle and are short of hands; we have asked them of you. Catastrophic epidemics will be in store for us, and we have employed you to help fill the gaps they leave. We have hostile neighbors to fight and a shortage of soldiers, and we have begged you to make us some. There are too many women and girls for our men, and we made you help us to cope with them. Among those women and children are some from whom we could not obtain children, and it is they we first offered to your embraces. We owe a regular due of men to a neighboring tyrant, and you and your companions will have helped us pay it; in five or six years' time we will send him your children, if they are worth less than ours. Robuster and healthier than you as we are, we realized at a first glance that you surpassed us in intelligence; and immediately we appointed some of our most beautiful wives and daughters to gather the seed of a superior race. It has been an experiment, and let us hope a successful one. We have extracted the sole profit that we could from you; and I would have you know that, though we are savages, we too know how to calculate. Go where you will, you will almost always find someone as sharp-witted as yourself. He will never give you anything unless it is no good to him and he always asks you for what is useful to himself. If he gives you a piece of gold for a piece of iron, it is because he places no value on gold and prizes iron.

But tell me, why are you not dressed like the others? What is the meaning of that long cloak which envelops you from head to foot, and that peaked bag you let hang on your shoulders or pull up round your ears?

THE CHAPLAIN

They tell you I a member of a body of men known in my country as "monks." The holiest of their vows is never to approach a woman and not to beget children.

OROU

So what do you do in the world?

THE CHAPLAIN

Nothing.

OROU

And your magistrates tolerate such a man, the worst kind of idler?

THE CHAPLAIN

They do even better; they respect him and ensure that he is respected.

OROU

The first thought I had was that nature, some accident, or a cruel custom had deprived you of ability to produce a fellow human, and that they had chosen to let you live and not kill you merely out of pity. But, my good monk, my daughter tells me you are a man, a man as vigorous as any Tahitian, and she hopes your many caresses will not be without fruit. Now I know, though, why yesterday night you cried out: "My religion! My calling!" But what I should like to know is why you monks receive such favor and respect from the powers-that-be?

THE CHAPLAIN

I don't know.

OROU

You can at least tell me why, being a man, you condemned yourself to not being one?

THE CHAPLAIN

It would take too long to explain.

OROU

And are monks always faithful to their vows of sterility?

THE CHAPLAIN

No.

OROU

I was sure of it. Do you also have female monks?

THE CHAPLAIN

Yes.

OROU

Are they as strict as male monks?

THE CHAPLAIN

They are more cloistered than the male ones; as a result they wither away through unhappiness or perish from boredom.

OROU

So Nature takes her revenge? Oh, what a frightful country! If everything is really as you say, you are worse barbarians than us.

The worthy Chaplain relates that he spent the rest of the day exploring the island and visiting huts, and that at evening, after supper, the father and mother begged him to sleep with the second of their daughters, Palli. She came to him in the same undress as Thia, and several times during the night he was heard to cry out: "But my religion! my calling!" The third night, he was troubled by the same scruples with Asto, the eldest; and, out of good manners, he bestowed the fourth night on his host's wife.

· V ·
Continuation of the Dialogue between *A* and *B*

A. I respect that decent Chaplain.
B. And I like the Tahitian customs, and Orou's conversation, much more.
A. It seems a little European in its style.
B. No doubt.

Here the worthy Chaplain complains of the shortness of his stay in Tahiti and thus the difficulty of getting to know the customs of its people—a people wise enough to have opted for mediocrity, favored enough by its climate to enjoy untroubled hours of ease, active enough to provide for all its basic needs, and indolent enough for its innocence, its tranquillity, and its happiness to be in no danger from the great leap forward of mind. Nothing, there, was branded as evil by public opinion or the law save what was evil in its intrinsic nature. Labor and the fruits of labor were in common. The word *property* was very little used; the passion of love, being reduced to a simple physical appetite, produced none of the turmoil that it does with us. The entire isle gave the appearance of one single great family, each hut corresponding, as it were, to a room in one of our great mansions. The Chaplain ends by declaring that the Tahitians will always live in his memory; that once back on board ship, he was tempted to strip off his clothes and return to spend his remaining days among them; and that he fears he may repent, quite often even, of his not having done so.

A. Nevertheless, what useful conclusions can we actually draw from the outlandish morals and manners of an uncivilized people?

B. They can remind us that, as soon as some physical cause—for instance the need to tame an ungrateful soil—spurs Man's ingenuity, his eagerness hurries him far beyond his goal; he is lost in the limitless ocean of his own fantasies. Long may the lucky Tahitian stay where he is now! Save in this remote nook of the globe, there has never been a true morality, and perhaps there never will be.

A. What do you mean by a "morality"?

B. I mean a universal submission to the laws, whether the laws are good or bad, and a behavior corresponding. If the laws are good, the morality will be a good one; if they are bad, the morality will be a bad one; but if the laws, whether bad or good, are not observed, you have the worst of all situations—that is to say, no morality at all. Now, how can you expect laws to be obeyed if they contradict one another? Search the annals of all ages and of all nations ancient or modern, and you will find Man subjected to three codes—the code of nature, the civil code, and the religious code—and compelled to break each of them in turn, since they never agree. From which it follows that what Orou said about our country is true of all: there has never been such a thing as a man, a citizen, or a man of religion.

A. Your theory, then—do I gather?—is that morality must be based on man's permanent and unchanging relationships, thus rendering religious law superfluous and requiring civil law to do no more than articulate the law of nature.

B. Yes, and any other system succeeds only in multiplying bad men, not in creating good ones.

A. Or that, if it is felt necessary to preserve all three codes, the two last should be faithful tracings of the first, which we carry graven in our hearts and will always be the strongest.

B. No, that is not quite right. All we have at birth is a similar constitution to other beings: the same needs, a bent toward the same pleasures, and an aversion to the same pains. This is what makes Man what he is and must be the basis of any suitable morality.

A. Though arriving at one is not easy.

B. Not so difficult either! For by following the rule of nature the most primitive of people, the Tahitians, seem to have come nearer to good legislation than any civilized nation.

A. Because it is easier for them to shed the worst of their rusticity than for us to retrace our steps or reform our abuses.

B. Especially those concerning the union of man with woman.

A. Perhaps. But let us begin at the beginning. Let us question Nature squarely and listen without prejudice to what she answers on this matter.

B. Certainly.

A. Does marriage exist in nature?

B. If by "marriage" you mean the preference a female gives to one male above all others or that a male gives to one female above all others—a mutual preference which results in a more or less lasting union, and perpetuates the species—then marriage is part of nature.

A. I think as you do; for one finds that preference not merely in the human species but in various animal ones—witness what we see in our countryside in springtime, a long cortege of males pursuing the same female, only one of whom will win the title of husband.

What are your thoughts about courtship?

B. If by "courtship" you mean the various means, energetic or delicate, that passion suggests to men and women to gain preference and to win the sweetest, most momentous, most universal of all enjoyments—then courtship is part of nature.

A. I agree with you; witness all the various attentions practiced by the male to please the female and by the female to provoke and fix the fancy of the male.

What about flirtation?

B. It is a lie which consists in pretending to a passion one does not feel, and promising a preference one has no intention of granting. The male flirt makes a fool of the female, the female flirt makes a fool of the male—a perfidious game which sometimes leads to the most disastrous consequences, an absurd charade in which deceiver and deceived are punished equally by the waste of the most precious instants of their life.

A. Thus, according to you, flirtation is not part of nature?

B. I don't say that.

A. And constancy?

B. I cannot improve on what Orou said about it to the Chaplain. Pathetic presumption on the part of two children who do not know themselves—blinded by the fever of a moment to the change and flux in all things round them!

A. And fidelity, that rare phenomenon?

B. Among us, almost always just well-meaning obstinacy and slow self-torture; in Tahiti, a chimera.

A. Jealousy?

B. The passion of a fearful and miserly animal; a feeling unworthy of Man; the fruit of our false morality and of the habit of treating thinking, feeling, willing, and free beings as so much legal property.

A. So jealousy, according to you, is not part of nature?

B. I don't say that. Everything—every vice, every virtue—is to be found in nature.

A. A jealous man is a gloomy man.

B. Like a tyrant, through knowing that he is one.

A. What about modesty?

B. This is becoming quite a Course in the Art of Love. Man does not like to be distracted or disturbed in his enjoyments. Making love is followed by a lassitude which would leave him at the mercy of his enemies. That's all that can be described as natural about modesty; the rest is pure convention. The Chaplain remarks, in a third section that I have not read to you, that the Tahitian does not blush before his daughters at the involuntary movements aroused in him by his wife's presence, and the daughters themselves may find the sight touching, but never embarrassing. But as soon as woman becomes the property of man and furtive enjoyment comes to be regarded as theft, we see the terms *modesty, reserve, propriety* arise, and with them imaginary virtues and vices: in a word, barriers between the two sexes, which often produce the very effect they are meant to curb, inflaming imaginations and provoking desires. When I see trees planted round our palaces, and women's dresses which half hide, half reveal their breasts, I seem to perceive a secret return to the forest and an appeal to the liberty of our ancient dwelling. The Tahitian would say: "Why are you hiding yourself? What are you ashamed of? Is it wrong to give way to the noblest impulse in all nature? Man: offer yourself frankly, if you wish to. Woman: if that man suits you, accept him with the same frankness."

A. Do not get too indignant. If we begin like civilized men, we usually finish up like a Tahitian.

B. Yes, but those conventional preliminaries waste half the life of a man of genius.

A. True. But does it matter that that "great leap forward" you said was so fatal should be slowed down?

A philosopher of our own day, when asked why men paid court to women and never women to men, replied that it was natural to ask of the one who was always in a position to give.

B. That answer has always seemed to me more clever than solid. Nature—call her indecent if you like—urges one sex toward the other without distinction; and in a primitive state of things, which one can imagine, though perhaps nowhere does it actually exist...

A. Not even in Tahiti?

B. No... the frontier between a man and a woman will be crossed by the more amorous of the two. If they lie in wait for each other, flee from each other, pursue each other, avoid each other, attack and defend themselves against each other, it is because passion, progressing at a different rate, is not working in them with the same force. So pleasure will spread, reach consummation, and fade on one side while it has hardly begun yet on the other, and both parties will be left sad. That is a true picture of what would happen between two young untrammeled creatures in a state of innocence. But when woman knows, from experience or education, the consequences—which are more or less cruel—of a moment's recklessness, her heart shudders at a man's approach. A man's heart does not shudder; his senses dictate to him and he obeys. A woman's senses speak to her also, but she refuses to listen, and it is the business of the man to quiet her fears and turn her head and seduce her. Man's natural impulsion toward women remains constant; woman's natural impulsion toward men is, as mathematicians would say, in direct proportion to passion and in inverse proportion to fear—a proportion complicated by innumerable factors in our societies, which foster the timidity of one sex and protract the other's pursuit. It is a species of military tactics, in which the resources for attack and the resources for defense keep abreast. Woman, by her resistance, acquires a halo, and man's violence attracts blame and odium; a violence which would be a trifle in Tahiti becomes a crime in our cities.

A. But how does it happen that an act so solemn in its purpose and urged upon us by Nature by the strongest of all attractions—that the greatest, sweetest, most innocent of pleasures—has become for us the greatest source of depravity and evil?

B. Orou gave the explanation ten times to the Chaplain. Listen once again, and try to remember.

It is because of the tyranny of Man, who has turned possession of a woman into a property right.

It is because of our morals and customs, which have loaded conjugal union with so many conditions.

It is because of our civil law, which complicates marriage by endless formalities.

It is because of the nature of our society, in which differences of rank and fortune dictate what is "done" and "not done."

It is because of a strange contradiction in all existing societies, by which the birth of a child, always an increase in wealth for the nation, will even more surely be an increase in poverty for the family.

It is because of the political temper of sovereigns, who look, in everything, for their own security and advantage.

It is because of religious teachings, which attach the name of vice and virtue to actions unconnected with morals.

How far from nature and happiness we have strayed! Nature's empire will never be destroyed; obstruct it as we will, it will endure. Write as often as you please on tablets of brass (to borrow the phrase of wise Marcus Aurelius) that the pleasurable friction of two intestines is a crime: man's heart will still be torn between that text and the violence of his own instincts. His rebellious heart will cry out continually; and a hundred times, in the course of a life, that grim inscription will fade from his sight. Inscribe on marble, "Thou shalt not eat of the flesh of the eagle or the ossifrage," "Thou shalt know no woman but thy wife," "Thou shalt not marry thy daughter"; make your penalties greater, the more bizarre your commandments; grow altogether ferocious; and *still* you will not alter my nature.

A. How brief our legal codes would be, if we strictly adhered in them to the code of nature. How many vices and errors Man would be spared!

B. Shall I tell you in brief the history of almost all our woe? It runs as follows. Once there was a natural man: inside that man there was installed an artificial man, and within the cave a civil war began which lasted the whole of his life. Sometimes the natural man gains the upper hand, sometimes he is worsted by the moral and artificial man; and in either case the poor monster is plagued, torn, tormented, and stretched on the rack. Forever groaning, forever unhappy is that monster, whether drunk with false dreams of glory or bowed to the earth with shame. Only extreme circumstances—but there are some—restore Man to his old simplicity.

A. Like poverty and illness, those two great exorcists?

B. You have named them. Let those arrive, and what happens to all that conventional virtue? In poverty, men lose all remorse; in illness, women lose their modesty.
A. I have noticed that.
B. But another phenomenon you may also have noticed is how, step by step with the progress from illness to convalescence and from convalescence to health, the artificial man returns. The moment when illness ceases is the moment when civil war breaks out again—though, for the moment, not to the advantage of the intruder.
A. Very true; I have noticed that myself. During convalescence the natural man is vigorous and can tame the artificial and moral one.

But tell me, finally: ought we to civilize Man, or should we leave him to his instinct?
B. Am I to give a straight answer?
A. Certainly.
B. Then, if your plan is to be a tyrant to him, go ahead and civilize him, poison him as thoroughly as you can with a morality contrary to nature; load him with fetters of every kind; obstruct his movements with a thousand obstacles; plague him with terrifying phantoms; perpetuate the war in the cave and see that the artificial man keeps his foot on the natural man's neck. But do you want man to be happy and free? Then do not interfere in his affairs; there are enough unexpected chances in the world to lead him to enlightenment or vice; and always remember that it was not for your sake but for theirs that cunning legislators molded and misshaped you as they have done. Look at all political, civil, and religious institutions; study them with care; and I much mistaken or you will find Man, century after century, the yoke-ox of a handful of knaves. Mistrust the man who comes to you praising "order"; creating order always means bullying others to their own discomfort. The Calabrians are almost the only people left, unseduced by the flattery of legislators.

A. And do you approve of the anarchy in Calabria?
B. I appeal to experience and will bet that their barbarity is less vicious than our urbanity. How many little villainies on our part, to balance those few great crimes of theirs we hear so much of! I think of uncivilized men as so many isolated cogwheels. If two of these wheels collide, one or other or both will, no doubt, get broken. So to prevent this, what did an individual, in his profound wisdom and sublime genius, do? He fitted those cogwheels together and made a machine of them; and in that machine, called "society," all the wheels were set in motion, rubbing one against the other and wearing one another out; and more got broken in a day, under the rule of law and order, than in a year in the anarchy of nature. And what a din, what havoc, what enormous destruction when two or three of those great machines violently collide!
A. So you prefer a brutal and primitive state of nature?
B. Upon my word, I do not know. But what I do know is: we often see the city dweller strip and return to the forest, but never a man of the forest put on clothes and resort to the city.
A. A thought has often occurred to me: that the sum of goods and evils may vary from individual to individual, but in an animal species the total sum of happiness or unhappiness may be unalterable. In which case, perhaps, all our efforts produce in the end as much harm as good. In a word, we are racking our brains to increase one term or other of an equation, when they stand to each other in a fixed and equal relation.

Nevertheless, I freely admit, the average life span of a civilized man is longer than that of a savage.
B. But must we assume the life span of a machine is in direct proportion to its wear and tear?
A. I see what it is; you are determined at all costs to believe men wickeder and more unhappy the more they are civilized.
B. I won't scour the globe to answer. I will say simply this. You will find man's condition a happy one only in Tahiti, and a bear-

able one only in a certain corner of Europe—a place where suspicious and wary governors have found how to keep mankind in a kind of numb passiveness.

A. You are thinking of Venice?[18]

B. Why not? You will hardly deny, at least, that nowhere does one find so little enlightenment, so little morality of the artificial kind, and so few unreal and phantasmal vices and virtues. All foreign visitors note the fact and commend it.

A. I did not expect to hear you praise that government.

B. Nor am I doing so. I am merely pointing out a certain compensation for slavery.

A. A poor enough compensation!

B. Perhaps. The Greeks proscribed the man who added a string to Mercury's lyre.[19]

A. And that ban of theirs is a bitter satire on the first lawmakers. It was the *first* string they should have cut.

B. You have seen my point. Wherever there is a lyre, there will be strings. Sophisticate natural appetites and you can expect to have wicked women.

A. Like Reymer.

B. And ruthless men.

A. Like Gardeil.

B. And innocent victims.

A. Like Tanié, Mademoiselle de la Chaux, the Chevalier Desroches, and Madame de la Carlière. You would look in vain in Tahiti for a depravity like that of the first two or misfortune like that of those others. So what shall we do? Are we to go back to Nature? Are we to submit to her laws?

B. What we must do is to speak against insane laws until they are reformed, but in the meantime to obey them. The man who, on his own authority, breaks a bad law encourages others to break good ones. It is better to be a madman among madmen than sane all on one's own. Let us tell ourselves, let us cry it aloud without cease, that shame, punishment, and ignominy have been attached to actions innocent in themselves; but let us not commit those actions, for shame, punishment, and ignominy are the worst of all evils. Let us imitate the worthy Chaplain and be a monk in France and a savage in Tahiti.

A. Don the garb of other countries when one goes there, but dress like one's neighbors at home.

B. Above all be honorable and sincere, to the point of scruple, with vulnerable creatures who cannot give us the boon we want from them without losing what, in our societies, are the most precious goods of all.

What has happened to that thick fog?

A. It has settled.

B. And shall we be free to please ourselves this afternoon, whether we go walking or stay at home?

A. That will depend, I imagine, somewhat more on the women than on us.

B. Those eternal women! One cannot walk a step without finding them in the way.

A. Shall we read them the conversation between the Chaplain and Orou?

B. What would they say about it, do you imagine?

A. I have no idea.

B. And what would they think about it?

A. Perhaps the opposite of what they say.

THE TWO FRIENDS FROM BOURBONNE

Once there were two men who might be called the Orestes and Pylades of Bourbonne. One was named Olivier, the other Felix. They were born on the same day, in the same house, being the children of two sisters. They had sucked the same milk, for one of the mothers had died in childbirth and the other had taken charge of both infants. They had been brought up together; their life had always been rather solitary; they loved each other in the same unthinking way that one breathes or that one exists; they felt it at every moment and had perhaps never once spoken of it. Once Felix, who thought himself a great swimmer, had been rescued from drowning by Olivier; neither of them remembered it. Felix had saved Olivier a hundred times from the perils his rash nature landed him in, and it never occurred to Olivier to thank him. They would return home in silence or talking about something else.

At the ballot for military service, the first of the fatal tickets fell to Felix, whereupon Olivier said: "The other one is mine." They served their term and returned to their native village. Whether they were dearer to each other than before I cannot tell you: for, my little brother, exchange of good deeds strengthens friendships of the thinking sort, but it may have no effect at all on what one might call domestic or "animal" ones. During a battle, when Olivier's head was about to be split by a saber, Felix had, automatically, put himself in the way and been scarred for life. It was said he was proud of this wound; I doubt it very much. At Hastenbeck,[1] Olivier had rescued Felix from under a pile of corpses. When questioned, they sometimes spoke of the help the other had given, never of the help they themselves had given. Olivier would say that Felix had done so-and-so, Felix that Olivier had done so-and-so; neither offered a word of praise.

A little while after their return, they fell in love, and, as chance would have it, with the same girl. It did not turn them into rivals; the first to realize the other's feelings withdrew. This was Felix. Olivier married the girl; and Felix, sick of life without knowing why, launched into all sorts of dangerous paths, the latest being smuggling.[2] You will be aware, dear boy, that there are four tribunals[3] in France—Caen, Rheims, Valence, and Toulouse—where smugglers are tried, and that the most severe of the four is at Rheims, where a man called Coleau,[4] the most ferocious soul ever formed by Nature, is presiding judge. Felix was arrested bearing firearms, brought before the terrible Coleau, and condemned to death, like five hundred before him. Olivier heard of Felix's plight. One night he leaves his wife's side and, without a word to her, sets off for Rheims. He gains access to Judge Coleau and throws himself at his feet, begging to be allowed to see and embrace Felix. Coleau looks at him, saying nothing for a moment, then gestures to him to sit down. Olivier does so. After half an hour Coleau takes out his watch and says to Olivier: "If you want to see and embrace your friend while he is still alive, you will have to hurry; he's on the road and, if my watch is right, will be hanged ten minutes from now." Olivier, transported with fury, gets up, deals Judge Coleau a staggering blow on the nape of the neck, nearly slaying him, rushes out to the public square, shouts, attacks the hangman, attacks the guards, and raises the People, already bitter against these executions. Stones fly; Felix is rescued and takes to his heels; and Olivier thinks how he can cover his retreat, but, though he has not noticed it, a soldier of the *maréchaussée*[5] has bayoneted him in the side. He reaches the city gate but can struggle no further. Some friendly wagoners haul him on to their cart, and they drop him at his own door just as he is breathing his last breath. He only has time to say, "Wife, come close, let me kiss you. I am dying, but the Man of the Scar is safe."

• • •

One evening we were taking a walk, as we often did, and saw, standing in front of a cottage, a tall woman with four little children at her feet. Her sad and determined expression caught our eye. After a moment she said to us: "You see these children. I am their mother, and I have no husband any more." This proud manner of demanding pity was designed to touch our hearts, and we offered her alms, which she accepted with dignity. This is how we learned the story of her husband, Olivier, and his friend, Felix. We spread the word about her and I hope did not do so in vain. The truth is, dear boy, that high qualities and greatness of soul are to be found in all conditions and in all lands; that a man may die obscure only for want of a better theater for his actions; and that one need not go to the Iroquois[6] to find two friends.

At the time when the brigand Testalunga[7] was infesting Sicily with his band, his friend and confidant Romano was taken prisoner. He was Testalunga's lieutenant and second-in-command. Romano's own father was arrested and imprisoned for various crimes and was offered pardon and liberty if Romano would betray his chief, Testalunga. The struggle between filial tenderness and sworn friendship was violent. The elder Romano, however, being ashamed to owe his life to treachery, persuaded his son to choose friendship. Romano agreed. His father was put to death; and the cruelest tortures were unable to make the son betray his accomplices.

You ask, my little brother, what happened to Felix. It's a natural curiosity, and the motive is so praiseworthy that we feel a little ashamed at not having felt it ourselves. To repair the fault, our thoughts first turned to M. Papin, doctor of theology, and curé of the church of Sainte-Marie in Bourbonne. Then Mama changed her mind, and we chose M. Aubert,[8] the Subdelegate, a good, kindly, straightforward man, who sent us the following account. You can rely on its truth.

"They said Felix is still alive. Having made his escape at Rheims he plunged into the nearby forests, for he knew every twist and turn from his smuggling days, and he tried to make his way back to Olivier's home, still not knowing what had happened to him.

"At the heart of a certain wood, where you have often gone walking, there lived a charcoal-burner, whose hut was used as a refuge by this smuggling tribe and which they also employed as a storehouse and an armory. Felix made his way here, narrowly escaping ambush by the guards who were at his heels. Some of his associates had brought word that he was in prison in Rheims, and the charcoal-burner and his wife were imagining he had been executed, when he appeared.

"I shall tell you the story as I heard it from the charcoal-burner's wife, who died here not long ago.

"It was her children, who were playing outside, who saw him first. As he lingered to kiss the youngest of them, his godchild, the rest went into the house crying: 'Felix! Felix!' Their father and mother came out, with the same joyful cry on their lips; but the poor fellow was so worn with fatigue and hunger that he had no strength to respond and fell almost fainting into their arms.

"The good people did what they could for him; they gave him bread and wine and vegetables from their garden; he ate and fell asleep.

"When he woke, his first words were about Olivier. 'Children, don't you know anything about Olivier?' — 'No,' they replied. He told them the whole affair at Rheims. He spent the next day and night with the family, sighing and murmuring the name 'Olivier.' He supposed Olivier was in prison in Rheims and wanted to go there, so that he could die at his side, and the charcoal-burner and his wife had great trouble in dissuading him.

"In the middle of the second night he took a musket, put a saber under his arm, and whispered: 'Charcoal-burner!' — 'Felix?' — 'Get your ax and follow me.' — 'Where to?' — 'Where do you think? To find Olivier.' So off they went. But as they came out of the forest they found themselves surrounded by the police.

"I am telling you what the charcoal-burner's wife told me, but it's incredible that two men on foot could have held their own as they did against a score of mounted police. Apparently these latter had spread out, hoping to take their quarry alive. Whatever the case, it was a fine melee; six of the horses were lamed, and seven of the horsemen received ax- or saber-wounds. The poor charcoal-burner fell with a bullet through his forehead. Felix got back into the forest, and, being incredibly agile, he rushed from one spot to another,[9] firing and charging his musket as he ran and emitting whistles. The whistles and the shots, coming at different intervals and from all sides, caused the police, in their terror, to imagine a whole horde of smugglers, and they beat a hasty retreat.

"When Felix saw they had gone, he returned to the scene of the battle, hoisted his companion's dead body on to his shoulder, and made his way back to the hut, where the charcoal-burner's wife and children were still asleep. He paused outside the door; he laid the corpse at his feet and sat down, with his back against a tree and his eyes upon the hut door. This was the spectacle that would await the charcoal-burner's wife when she came out of her poor dwelling.

"She wakes up; she finds her husband is not beside her; she looks round for Felix—no Felix. She gets up, she goes out; she sees, utters a cry, and falls over backward. Her children rush to her; they see and cry out too; they hurl themselves, sprawling, on their father and on their mother. The charcoal-burner's wife, brought to by her children's screams, tears her hair and gouges her cheeks. Felix, motionless at the foot of the tree, with eyes fast shut and head thrown back on his shoulders, murmurs: 'Kill me! Children, for pity's sake, kill me!'

"They spent three days and nights in such lamentation. On the fourth day Felix says to the charcoal-burner's wife: 'Woman, take your pack, put in some bread, and follow me.' After long circling through our mountains and forests they reached Olivier's house, which stands, as you know, on the outskirts of the town at the point where the highway forks, one road leading to Franche-Comté and the other to Lorraine.

"Here is where Felix had to learn of Olivier's death and find himself among the widows of two men, both of them massacred on his own behalf. He went in and asked brusquely of Olivier's wife: 'Where is Olivier?' From her silence, her costume, and her tears he realized that his friend was no more. Stricken, he fell, gashing his head on the kneading trough. The two women picked him up, his blood spattering all over them. As they stanched his wound with their aprons, they heard him say: 'You were their wives, and you help me!!' He fainted, then recovered consciousness, sighing: 'Why did he not just abandon me? Why did he have to come to Rheims? Why did you let him come?' Then he went out of his mind, raged, and rolled on the ground tearing his clothes. In one of his fits he seized his saber and was about to kill himself, when the women threw themselves on him, shouting for help, and neighbors rushed on the scene. They tied him up, and he was bled seven or eight times; the fury of his madness eventually diminished through sheer exhaustion, and he lay like a dead man for three or four days. Thereupon his reason returned. For a moment he stared around, as if emerging from a deep sleep, and asked: 'Where am I? You women, who are you?' One of them answered 'I am the charcoal-burner's wife.' 'Ah yes, I remember... And you...?' Olivier's wife was silent. Then he fell weeping. He turned his face to the wall, exclaiming between sobs: 'I am at Olivier's... This bed is Olivier's... And that woman was his wife!... Ah!...'

"The two women took such tender care of him, they aroused so much pity in him, they begged him so earnestly to live, and insisted so touchingly that he was their sole resource, that he listened to them.

"All the remaining time he lived in that house he never went to bed. At nighttime he would go out and would roam the fields and roll upon the ground, calling upon Olivier. One or other of the women would follow him and bring him back at daybreak.

"A number of people knew he was in that house, and not all were well disposed toward him. The two widows warned him of his danger. It was the afternoon; he was sitting at a table, with a saber on his lap, his head propped on his elbows, and his fists over his eyes. At first he made no reply. Olivier's wife had a son of about seventeen or eighteen years of age; the charcoal-burner's wife had a daughter who was fifteen. All of a sudden he said to the charcoal-burner's wife: 'Go and find your daughter and bring her here.' He possessed some hay and he sold it. The charcoal-burner's wife returned with her daughter, and Olivier's son married her. Felix gave them the money from his hay, kissed them, and, with tears, asked them for their pardon; and they went to set up house in the humble cottage where they are still to be found and where they act as father and mother to the other children. The two widows lived on together, and thus Olivier's children gained a father and two mothers. (The charcoal-burner's wife died about a year and a half ago and Olivier's widow still mourns her loss every day.)

"One evening, while the two widows were spying on Felix—for one or other of them kept their eyes on him all the time—they saw him burst into tears. Silently he stretched out his arms toward their door, then he set to work packing his bag. They said nothing, for they knew how necessary it was for him to go. The three ate their supper in silence. In the middle of the night he got up; the women were not asleep; he tiptoed toward the door. Pausing, he gazed at the two women's bed, dried his eyes with one hand, and went out. The two women held each other more tightly and passed the rest of the night in tears. No one knows where he took refuge; but few weeks passed without his sending them money.

"The forest where the charcoal-burner's daughter lives with Olivier's son belongs to a certain M. le Clerc de Ranconnière, a very wealthy man and lord of the manor of another village in this vicinity, called Courcelles. One day, when M. de Ranconnière (or de Courcelles, whichever you like to call him) was hunting in the forest, he reached Olivier's son's cottage. He went in; he began playing with the children, who are pretty creatures; he questioned them; the wife's face, not an uncomely one, pleased him; the firm tones of the husband, who had a lot of his father in him, interested him; he learned the story of their parents; he promised to try to obtain a pardon for Felix and was successful.

"Felix passed into the service of M. de Ranconnière, who gave him employment him as a gamekeeper.

"He had been living for two years or so in the chateau of Ranconnière, sending the widows a substantial portion of his wages, when his devotion to his master and his own proud character involved him in an affair which was nothing to begin with but led to terrible trouble.

"M. de Ranconnière had for neighbor at Courcelles a certain Monsieur Fourmont,[10] Presidial Councillor at Lh... Their two houses were only separated by a boundary stone. This stone obstructed M. de la Ranconnière's doorway and made it difficult for carriages to enter. He had it moved a few feet in M. Fourmont's direction; the latter moved it an equal distance in M. de la Ranconnière's direction; and there ensued hatred, insults, and a lawsuit between the two neighbors. The boundary-stone dispute led to several other more serious ones. Matters were at this point when, one evening, as M. de la Ranconnière and his gamekeeper Felix were returning from hunting, they encountered M. Fourmont and his brother, an army officer, on the highroad. The latter said to his brother: 'What do you say to giving that old goat's face a cut or two?' M. de la Ranconnière did not hear the remark, but unfortunately Felix did and, in a haughty voice, said: 'Sir, if you have the courage, why not try?' So saying he threw down his musket and grasped the hilt of his saber—for he went nowhere without his saber. The young officer drew his sword and approached. M. de la Ranconnière hurried up to intervene and seized his protector round the body, but meanwhile the military man picked up Felix's musket and fired it at him, missing him. Felix responded with a swing of his saber, which sent the young man's sword flying and with it half his arm; and the result was a criminal trial as well as three or four civil ones. Felix lay in jail, there was a long and frightening judicial process, and the upshot was a magistrate stripped of his office and more or less disgraced, an officer dismissed from his regiment, M. de la Ranconnière dead from grief, and Felix, still in prison, exposed to the full resentment of the Fourmonts. He would have come to a grim end if love had not come to his rescue. The jailer's daughter conceived a passion for him and helped him to escape. (If that is not the true story, it is at least the one that is generally told.)

"Felix went off to Prussia, where he is still serving in a guards regiment. They say he is much loved by his comrades and has even become known to the King. His nom de guerre is 'Man of Sorrow.' Olivier's widow tells me he still supports her.

"So, Madame, I have told you all I could find of Felix's story. I am enclosing a letter from Monsieur Papin, our local curé. I don't know what is in it; but I am afraid that the poor priest, who is a little narrow in his views, and queer-tempered into the bargain, may speak of Olivier and Felix according to his own prejudices. I beg you, Madame, to listen simply to the facts, which you may depend on as true, and to the goodness of your own heart, which will instruct you better than the most eminent casuist of the Sorbonne—which M. Papin is not."

LETTER
From M. PAPIN, Doctor in Theology and curé of Sainte-Marie at Bourbonne.

I do not know, Madame, what Monsieur the Subdelegate may have told you about Olivier and Felix, nor what interest you can take in two brigands, whose every step through the world has left a trace of blood. Providence, which has punished one of them, has granted the other a moment's respite, which I very much fear he will not profit by. But God's will be done! I know that there are people here, and it would not surprise me to find that Monsieur the Subdelegate was one of them, who speak of these two men as models of a rare friendship. But in the eyes of God what is even the most sublime virtue in the absence of piety, of the respect due to the church and its ministers, and submission to the Sovereign's laws? Olivier died at the door of his own house, without benefit of the sacraments. When I was summoned to Felix by the two widows, I could get nothing out of him but the name "Olivier": no trace of religion, no sign of repentance. I do not remember ever seeing him at the tribunal of penitence. Olivier's wife is an arrogant woman whom I have had reason to complain of more than once. On the pretext that she can read and write, she believes herself fitted to teach children; and they are to be seen neither at the parish schools, nor at my own classes. Madame may judge from this whether individuals of such a type are worthy of her kindness! The Gospel continually exhorts us to show pity toward the poor; but the merit of one's charity is doubled if one chooses the right poor; and no one is better placed to know the truly needy than a pastor who ministers to the needy and the rich alike. If Madame would deign to honor me with her trust, I could perhaps direct the tokens of her benevolence in a manner more useful to the unfortunate and more meritorious for herself.

I am, with great respect, etc.

Madame de *** thanked M. the Subdelegate Aubert for his

kind attentions and sent her alms to M. Papin with the following note.

I am greatly obliged to you, Monsieur, for your wise advice. I will confess that I felt moved by the story of those two men; and you will admit that so rare a friendship was well fitted to seduce an honnête *and feeling soul. But you have cleared my mind for me, and I have realized it may be more proper to succor chastened and Christian virtues than natural and pagan ones. I beg you to accept the modest sum that I am sending you and to distribute it according to a more enlightened conception of charity than mine.*

I have the honor to be, etc.

As may readily be guessed, Olivier's widow and Felix received no share of Madame de ***'s charity. Felix died; and the poor woman and her children would have perished in destitution if she had not taken refuge in the woods with her eldest son, where she lives a life of toil, despite her great age, and subsists among her children and grandchildren as best she can.

• • •

And then there are two sorts of story — *There are many more than that,* you will tell me — Oh very well. But I have in mind the story in the style of Homer, Virgil, and Tasso, which I will call the tale of marvels. Here Nature is exaggerated; truth is hypothetical, and if the storyteller takes care to be faithful to his chosen "module," if everything in the action and the speeches corresponds to it, he has attained the degree of perfection the genre of his work calls for, and there is nothing more you can ask of him. In entering in his poem, you are setting foot in an unknown country, where nothing happens as it does in the one you live in yourself, but where everything takes place on a grand scale, as the things done around you take place on a petty one.... Then there is the tale of entertainment, in the style of La Fontaine, Vergier,[11] Ariosto, and Hamilton,[12] where the storyteller proposes neither the imitation of nature, nor truth, nor illusion; he sets off into imaginary space. Tell him: "Be gay, ingenious, varied, original, even extravagant if you wish; but seduce me by details, so that the charm of the form will always conceal from me the improbability of the content"; and if the storyteller has done these things that you have asked of him, he has done everything.... Finally there is the historical tale, as we find it in the novels of Scarron, Cervantes, and so on. — *The devil take the historical tale, and the historical storyteller! He is a tedious and uninspired liar.* — Yes, if he does not know his trade. This kind of storyteller sets out to deceive you, while sitting at your own fireside; the ideal he is aiming at is rigorous truth; he wants to be believed; he wants to be interesting, touching, exciting, moving; he wants to make your flesh shudder and your tears flow, effects which cannot be obtained without eloquence and without poetry. But eloquence is a source of falsehood, and nothing is more destructive of illusion than poetry; both exaggerate, aggrandize, overdo things generally, and provoke mistrust. So how will this storyteller go about deceiving you? In the following way: he will sprinkle his narrative with such relevant little circumstances, with strokes so simple and natural and yet so difficult to imagine, that they make you say to yourself: "Good heavens, that must be true; no one could have invented a thing like that." It is in this way that he will redeem the exaggeration of eloquence and poetry, that the truth of nature will ratify the conjuring-tricks of art, and that he will satisfy two apparently contradictory demands: to be at one and the same time a historian and a poet, a truth-teller and a liar. An example borrowed from another art will perhaps make clearer what I mean. A painter executes a head on a canvas; all its forms are strong, grand, and regular; it is the most perfect and rare ensemble. In examining it I feel respect, admiration, and awe; I search for the model of it in nature and cannot find it; by comparison with it everything is feeble, meager, and trivial. I tell myself that, yes, it is an idealized head... But let the artist cause me to see on the forehead of that head a tiny scar, a wart on one of its temples, an imperceptible cut in the lower lip, and from being an idealization it becomes a portrait; let there be a smallpox mark at the corner of the eye or beside the nose, and this woman's face is no longer the face of Venus, it is the portrait of one of my neighbors. So I shall tell our historical storytellers: "Your faces are beautiful, well and good; but what is lacking is the wart on the temple, the cut on the lip, the smallpox mark at the side of the nose which would render them true"; and as my friend the actor Cailleau[13] would say: "a little dust on my shoes, and I am not coming out of my dressing room but returning from the countryside."

Atque ita mentitur, sic veris falsa remiscet,
Primo ne medium, medio ne discrepet imum.
Hor. *Ars poet,* 151–52

And then a little moralizing, after a little aesthetics, an excellent combination! Felix was a poor beggar with no worldly goods; Olivier was another poor beggar with no worldly goods; you can say the same of the charcoal-burner and the charcoal-burner's wife and the other characters in this tale and may well decide that, as a rule, total and solid friendships can only occur between men who have no worldly goods: in such cases a man is his friend's entire fortune, and his friend is his likewise. Hence the truth of the observation that ill-fortune strengthens bonds, and here is matter for an extra paragraph for the first edition of Helvetius's *Treatise on the Human Mind.*[14]

CONVERSATION OF A FATHER WITH HIS CHILDREN

or

The Danger of Setting Oneself above the Law

My father,[1] a pious man but nevertheless a person of excellent judgment, had won a great reputation in his locality by his probity. He was more than once chosen as arbitrator between his fellow citizens, and people he had never met would appoint him as executor of their dying wishes. At his death, the poor mourned his loss greatly. During his last illness, grand folk and humble were as troubled as one another. When the word went round that he was nearing his end, the whole town was in distress. His image will live in my memory always. I seem to see him in his armchair, with that tranquil air of his and that look of serenity; I can still hear his voice. Here is the story of one of our evenings, a model of how we spent many others.

It was winter. We three, my brother the abbé, my sister,[2] and myself, were sitting round my father in front of the fire. He said to me—we had been having a conversation about the discomforts of fame—"My son, we have both made a lot of noise in the world: with this difference, that the noise you made with your tools ruined your own rest while the noise I made with mine only ruined other people's." After that little joke, for what it was worth, the old cutler fell into a reverie, gazing at us with a look full of meaning. "What are you thinking about, Papa?" asked the abbé? "I was thinking," he replied, "how a reputation as a man of principle, though the best kind there is, has its dangers, even for someone who deserves it." Then, after a brief pause, he added: "I still shudder when I think of it... Would you believe it, my children: there was a moment when I was on the point of ruining you all—yes, ruining you utterly."

THE ABBÉ

How was that?

MY FATHER

How? Like this. — But before I begin, Soeurette (he said to his daughter), see to my cushion for me, it has slipped down. Denis (he said to me) pull my dressing gown round my legs, the fire is roasting them. — You all knew the curé at Thivet?[3]

MY SISTER

That good old priest who, at the age of a hundred, walked his twelve miles every morning?

THE ABBÉ

And who died at a hundred and one on hearing that his ninety-nine-year-old brother, who lived with him, was dead?

MY FATHER

The very same.

THE ABBÉ

Well?

MY FATHER

Well, his heirs, who were poor folk, getting a living wherever they could, begging on the highroads or in church porches, sent me a deed of attorney, authorizing me to present myself and take charge of their dead relative, the curé's, effects. How could I refuse to paupers a service I had done for so many wealthy families! I went to Thivet, I summoned the local men of law, I had seals affixed, and I waited for the heirs' arrival. They were not long in coming. There were about ten or twelve of them: women without stockings, without shoes, practically without clothes, clasping children to their bosoms wrapped in their dirty aprons; old men in tatters dragging their way along the highroad, with a stick and a bundle of rags, wrapped in another rag, on their shoulders—the most hideous spectacle of poverty you could hope to see. So imagine the joy of these heirs at the prospect of ten thousand or so francs apiece; for according to local reports the curé's estate amounted to at least a hundred thousand francs. The seals were broken, and I spent the day making an inventory. Night fell, the poor wretches found somewhere to sleep, and I was left alone. I was in a hurry to put them in possession and be rid of them, so that I could get back to my own affairs. On the floor under the bureau I found an old strongbox without a lid, full of papers of every kind. There were old letters, drafts of replies to them, ancient receipts and the stubs of the curé's own receipts, lists of expenses, and other such useless stuff; but in such a case one has to read everything, one can neglect nothing. I was nearing the end of the tedious business when I came on a longish document, and what do you think it was? A will! A will signed by the curé! A will so old that that the executors named in it had been dead for twenty years! A will in which he left nothing to those poor wretches sleeping round me and named the Frémins,[4] wealthy Paris booksellers—you will have heard of them—as residuary legatee. I leave you to imagine my surprise and distress. For what was I to do with the thing? Ought I to burn it? Why not? Did it not bear all the signs of having been thrown away? And then, the place where I found it, and the papers it was mixed up with: surely they testified against it, quite apart from its own revolting injustice? That was what I kept saying to myself; and, picturing the misery of those poor defrauded wretches, I gently advanced the will toward the fire. Then other thoughts supervened. Terror of making a mistake in such an important case, distrust of my own judgment, fear that the voice of pity was deafening me to the voice of justice suddenly seized me and held my hand; and I spent the rest of the night pondering that iniquitous document, holding it over the flames again several times, undecided whether to burn it or not. Eventually I decided for the latter. A minute before or after it might have been the former. In my perplexity I thought it wise to ask advice, so when dawn broke, I got on my horse and hurried back to town. I passed my own door without stopping and went on to the seminary, which at that time was run by the Oratorians, among them a priest famous for enlightenment and saintliness. This was Father Bouin. He left a reputation in the diocese as the greatest casuist ever known.

My father had got thus far when Doctor Bissei entered the room. Bissei was the family doctor and also a family friend. He inquired after my father's health, took his pulse, changed his diet this way, changed it that way, found a chair, and joined our conversation.

My father asked after some of his patients, among them the rascally old steward of M. de la Mesangère, onetime *maire* of our town. This steward had made a disgraceful mess of his master's affairs, had fraudulently borrowed money in his name, made away with title-deeds, and stolen from his funds. He had committed an infinity of rogueries, most of them proved beyond doubt, and he was about to be sentenced to some degrading penalty, if not to death. The whole neighborhood was buzzing with the story. The Doctor told my father that the man was very ill, but he did not despair of saving him.

MY FATHER

That would be to do him a very ill service.

MYSELF

And to perform a very ill deed.

DR. BISSEI

A very ill deed! Why so?

MYSELF

There are enough scoundrels in the world without preserving ones who want to get out of it.

DR. BISSEI

My business is to heal people, not to judge them. I will heal him because it is my profession, and then the magistrate can hang him, that being his.

MYSELF

Doctor, there is a certain obligation common to all citizens—to you as to me. It is to work with all our strength for the good of the republic; and restoring health to a wrongdoer, from whom the law is about to deliver the republic, can hardly be so described.

DR. BISSEI

But whose job is it to decide he is a wrongdoer? Is it mine?

MYSELF

No. But, Doctor, let me change the case a little. Let us suppose a patient whose crimes are publicly notorious. You are called in; you rush to his bedside; you open the curtains and recognize Cartouche or Nivet.[5] Will you heal Cartouche or Nivet?

Doctor Bissei, after a moment's hesitation, replied firmly that he would heal him; that he would forget the patient's name and concentrate on the nature of his illness; that this was the only thing he was allowed to know about; that if he went a single step beyond it, he would very soon not know where to stop; that if a doctor's prescription had to be preceded by an examination of the patient's life and morals, men's lives would be at the mercy of ignorance, passion, and prejudice. What you say about Nivet a Jansenist would say to me about a Molinist and a Catholic about a Protestant. If you want me banned from the bed of a Cartouche, a fanatic will want me banned from the bed of an atheist. It's enough to have to measure out medicine, without having to measure what degree of wickedness allows it to be, or not to be, administered.

MYSELF

But Doctor if, after your brilliant cure, the first use the criminal makes of his convalescence is to murder a friend of yours, what will you say? Put your hand on your heart; wouldn't you repent of having cured him? Would you not ask yourself bitterly, "Why did I help him? Why did I not let him die?" Would this thought not be enough to poison the rest of your days?

DR. BISSEI

I should certainly be consumed with grief, but I would not feel remorse.

MYSELF

But what remorse would you feel, not at having killed a mad dog, it's not a question of that, but of having let it die? Doctor, listen to me. Suppose me braver than you; suppose I do not let myself be bound by futile reasonings. Imagine me a doctor. I look at my patient and recognize a criminal. I would speak to him thus: "Wretched fellow, make haste and die; it will be the best thing for others and for you too. I know very well what should be done to cure the pain in your side, but I do not intend to prescribe it; I do not hate my fellow citizens enough to send you back among them and prepare eternal sorrow for myself by the new crimes you will commit. I will not be your accomplice. They would punish a person who hid you in their home; am I to consider a person who saves your life innocent? No, that cannot be. If I have any regret, it is that, in handing you over to death, I am saving you from worse punishment. I shall not strive to restore the life of a man whom natural equity, the good of society, and the welfare of my fellowmen call upon me to denounce. Die, and let it not be said that, through my science and skill, the world has one more monster."

DR. BISSEI

So how are we, Papa? Now you know the rule. Not so much coffee after dinner, do you hear?

MY FATHER

Ah, Doctor, coffee is so good!

DR. BISSEI

At all events, plenty, *plenty,* of sugar.

MY SISTER

But Doctor, sugar will heat his blood.

DR. BISSEI

Stuff and nonsense, my dear. Goodbye, Philosopher.

MYSELF

One more word, Doctor. Galen, who lived under Marcus Aurelius, and who certainly was no ordinary man, though he believed in dreams and amulets and black magic, said this about his rules for the care of newborn children: "I address my remarks to Greeks and Romans and to all those who follow in their footsteps on the road to knowledge. But as for Germans, and the rest of the barbarians, they are no more worthy to hear them than bears, wild boars, lions, or other brute beasts."[6]

DR. BISSEI

I knew that, and you are both of you in the wrong: he for offering such an absurd opinion, and you for regarding him as an authority. You would not exist, your eulogy or critique of Galen would never have existed, if Nature had not had her own secret, and a better one than his, for preserving the children of Germans.

MYSELF

During the last plague in Marseilles[7]...

DR. BISSEI

Be quick. I am in a hurry.

MYSELF

... there were brigands who raided the houses, pillaging, slaughtering, and exploiting the general disorder to enrich themselves by all sorts of crimes. One of the brigands caught the plague and was recognized by one of the gravediggers whom the authorities had ordered to dispose of the dead. These latter went into houses and threw the corpses out into the street. The gravedigger, looking at the criminal, said to him: "Ah, so it's you, you devil"; and he seized him by the feet and dragged him toward the window. The criminal cried: "I'm not dead!" "You are dead enough for me," replied the other, as he pitched him out of the third story. Doctor, I tell you: in my eyes that gravedigger, who so neatly disposed of the plague-stricken rogue, would have less to blame himself for than a skillful physician like you who cured him. So good evening.

DR. BISSEI

My dear Philosopher, I will admire your great mind and your warm heart as much as you please; but your morality is not mine, nor, I wager, will it be the abbé's.

THE ABBÉ

You have won your wager.

I was going to take the abbé on, when my Father said to me with a smile: "You are arguing against your own cause."

MYSELF

How so?

MY FATHER

You want that rascal of a steward dead, don't you? Well then, leave him in the Doctor's hands... Did I hear you whisper something?

MYSELF

I was saying that Bissei will never deserve the inscription that, when Hadrian the Sixth[8] died, the Romans placed above his doctor's door: TO THE LIBERATOR OF THE FATHERLAND.

MY SISTER

And if he had been Cardinal Mazarin's physician, the wagoners would not have said of him, as they did of Guénaut,[9] "Comrades, let the Doctor pass. It's he who did us the favor of killing the Cardinal."

My father smiled again and said: "Where had I got to in my story?"

MY SISTER

You had gone to see Father Bouin.

MY FATHER

Yes, I explained the whole affair to him. He replied: "Nothing could be more to your credit, Sir, than your feelings of pity for those unfortunate heirs. Suppress the will, come to their aid, you have my full approval; but on one condition, that you yourself reimburse the residuary legatee with the full amount, neither more nor less, that you have deprived him of." ... But I can feel a draft round my shoulders. The Doctor must have left the front door open. Soeurette, go and shut it.

MY SISTER

Yes, Papa; but I hope you won't go on with your story until I get back.

MY FATHER

Of course.

My sister, who was away for a little while, exclaimed on returning, with a touch of pique: "I was held up by that idiot who pinned two notices on his door, one of them reading 'House for sale for 20,000 francs or to let for 1,200 francs a year' and the other, 'Loan of 20,000 francs on offer for one year, at 6 percent.' "

MYSELF

Idiot, Soeurette? But what if there had only been one notice instead of two, and the loan notice were just another version of the "To let" one. But let's forget that and return to Father Bouin.

MY FATHER

Father Bouin went on: "Anyway, who authorized you to give sanction or otherwise to legal documents? Who authorized you to interpret the intentions of the dead?" — "But Father Bouin... the box!" — "Who authorized you to decide if the will had been put there to get rid of it or just got there by accident? Has nothing like that ever happened to you? Have you never had to retrieve a precious paper you had thrown into the wastepaper basket?" — "But Father Bouin: the date of the will, and its being such a disgraceful one?" — "Who authorized you to pronounce on its disgracefulness or otherwise, or to decide the bequest must be illicit, when it could be some kind of restitution or have some other honorable purpose?" — "But Father Bouin: the immediate heirs being so poor and those remote ones so rich?" — "Who authorized you to weigh what the deceased owed to his close relatives, whom you don't know, against what he owed to his legatee, whom you don't know either?" — "But Father Bouin, what about that pile of letters from the legatees, which the deceased had not even bothered to open?... I forgot to tell you (my Father added) that in that mass of papers among which I found the fatal testament, there were twenty, thirty, I don't know how many letters from the Frémins, all still sealed." — "There's nothing in any of this (said Father Bouin): neither the box, nor the letters, nor '*But,* Father Bouin...' nor '*If,* Father Bouin...' No one has the right to infringe the law or offer to read the mind of the dead or dispose of other people's property. If Providence has decided to chastise the heir or the legatee or the deceased, for it could be any of them, by the accidental survival of this will, the fact must be faced."

After a verdict as clear and definite as this, from the most enlightened of our local clergy, I was left bemused and trembling, wondering what would have become of me, and of you too my children, if I had in fact burned the will, as I had been on the point of doing ten times, and had been tormented by scruples later and had gone to consult Father Bouin. I would have repaid the money—oh most certainly I would have repaid it!—and you would have been ruined.

MY SISTER

But, Father: then you had to return to the old curé's house and announce to that band of paupers that there was nothing for them and they were to go away the same as they had come. With such a feeling heart as yours, how were you able to face it?

MY FATHER

Upon my word, I don't know. In the first instant, I thought of giving up my power of attorney and having myself replaced by a man of law; but a man of law would have acted with absolute strictness and sent those poor folk packing without more ado, whereas I could do something to alleviate their lot. So I returned to Thivet the same day. My sudden and mysterious absence had caused some uneasiness, and the sad look on my face when I returned caused considerably more. However, I kept control of myself, I concealed my feelings as best I could.

MYSELF

That is to say, exceedingly badly.

MY FATHER

As a first step, I put all the valuables in a place of safety. I assembled a certain number of townsfolk in the house, to give help if necessary. I opened the wine cellar and the barns and gave those poor wretches the run of them, encouraging them to drink and eat and share out the wine and corn and all other consumables.

THE ABBÉ

But Father!...

MY FATHER

I know; it belonged to them no more than the rest.

MYSELF

Abbé, for Heaven's sake, don't interrupt!

MY FATHER

Eventually there I was, pale as death, trembling, opening my mouth and shutting it again, sitting down, standing up, beginning sentences I could not finish, weeping—and round me all those people crying: "What's the matter, Sir, what's the matter?" — "What's the matter?" I groaned.... "A will... A will which disinherits you." These few words cost me so much to say that I nearly fainted.

MY SISTER

I can understand that.

MY FATHER

What a scene followed, what a scene! I shudder when I recall it. I can still hear those cries of grief and fury and rage and the wild curses. (Here my father covered his eyes and ears.) Those women, those women! I can see them now: some rolling on the ground, tearing their hair; some gouging their cheeks and breasts; some foaming at the mouth and swinging their children by the feet, ready to dash their skulls on the pavement if not prevented. The men broke and overturned and demolished everything they could lay their hands on; they threatened to set the house on fire; others, raving, scrabbled at the ground as if to dig up the curé's corpse and tear it apart; and all through this din the shrill screams of the children, sharing in their parents' despair, without knowing why, and pelted with blows as they clutched at their garments. I do not think I have ever suffered so much in my whole life.

Meanwhile I had written to the legatee in Paris. I explained the whole business to him, and I pressed him to respond speedily, to avoid any further accident.

I had managed to calm the unfortunate heirs a little by the hope, which I was in fact nursing, of persuading the legatee to renounce his rights, or at least to interpret them generously, and I had dispersed them to cottages on the farthest outskirts of the village.

The Frémin from Paris arrived. I studied his looks, which were hard-faced and boded little good.

MYSELF

Great shaggy black eyebrows, tiny furtive eyes, a big mouth with a twist in it, and a swarthy complexion covered in pockmarks?

MY FATHER

Exactly. It had hardly taken him thirty hours to come the sixty leagues. I began by showing him the poor wretches whose cause I would be pleading. They stood before him in silence, the women weeping, the men meekly leaning on their sticks, bonnet in hand. Frémin sat with his eyes shut and his chin on his chest, paying them no attention. I spoke in their favor with all the force at my command: where does one find the things one says on such occasions? I insisted on how uncertain it was that the inheritance was actually valid; I appealed to him in the name of his own wealth and the spectacle of poverty before him; I may actually have thrown myself at his feet. Not a farthing could I wring out of him. He replied that all these matters were irrelevant; that a will existed, and he was not interested in its past history; that he attached more importance to what I had done than to what I said. In a fury I hurled the keys in his face. He picked them up and took possession of everything, and I returned home so troubled, so distressed, so altered that your mother (she was still living then) imagined I had suffered some terrible disaster... Ah, children, what a man, that Frémin!

After this story we sat silent, meditating, each in our own way, on this strange affair. Then visitors began to arrive. First a clergyman, a fat Prior, I forget his name: he was a sounder expert on wine than he was on ethics and better acquainted with Verville's merry *Tales* than with the *Theological Monthly.*[10] Next a man of the law, a notary and *lieutenant de police* named Dubois;[11] and a little after him, a workman who had something special to say to my father. We invited him in, and with him a retired civil engineer with a taste for mathematics, a subject he had once taught. He was one of the workman's neighbors. The workman himself was a hatter.

The hatter began by saying there were rather too many people present for what he wanted to discuss. So everyone left, except the Prior, the man of law, the mathematician, and myself, since the hatter asked us to stay.

"Monsieur Diderot," he said to my Father, glancing round the room to make sure he was not overheard, "it is your great probity and wisdom which bring me here; and I am happy, too, to meet these other gentlemen, all of whom I know, though perhaps they do not know me. A priest, a man of law, a scholar, a philosopher, and a man of good will! With persons of such different callings, all so honorable and enlightened, I should be unlucky not to find the advice I need. But promise me, in the first place, to keep my affair a secret, whatever course I decide on." We promised, and he continued. "I have no children. I had none by my last wife, whom I lost about a fortnight ago. Since that time I have not known what to do with myself: I have been unable to drink or eat or work or sleep. I get up, I dress, I go out, I roam round the village devoured by care. For eighteen years I looked after my wife, who was sick; I did everything required of me, all the things that her illness made necessary. What I spent on her consumed every penny that came into the house and has left me burdened with debts. In a word, when I die, worn out and with all my best years wasted, I should be no more forward in the world than on the day I first set up in business, if I were to obey the law—that is to say, if I let her relatives have what is due to them from her dowry. She brought with her a splendid trousseau; for her father and mother, who loved their daughter dearly, did everything they could for her, indeed more than they really could. There were quantities of fine clothes, still more or less unused, for the poor woman was not given the chance to wear them; also twenty thousand francs in cash, the proceeds of a note repaid by M. Michelin, the deputy procurer-general. As soon as I had closed her eyes, I took possession of the clothes and money. Gentlemen, now you know my situation. Have I done right, or have I done wrong? My conscience is not clear. I seem to hear a voice saying: 'You are a thief. Give it all back, give it back!' What is your opinion? Remember, Sirs, that my wife, when she passed away, had taken everything I had earned in twenty years; that I am scarcely able to work now; that I am in debt; and that if I make restitution, there will be nothing for me but the poorhouse—if not today, then tomorrow. Give me your views, Sirs; I want them. Must I make restitution and go to the poorhouse?"

"Honor where honor is due," said my Father, bowing toward the priest. "Monsieur the Prior, it is for you to speak."

"My child," said the Prior to the hatter, "I do not like scruples, they bother one's head and do no good to anyone. Perhaps you ought not to have taken that money; but since you did, my advice is to keep it."

MY FATHER

Monsieur Prior, that can hardly be your last word?

THE PRIOR

Certainly it is. That's as far as my ideas will take me.

MY FATHER

Which is not very far. Your turn, Monsieur the Magistrate.

THE MAGISTRATE

My friend, you are in an awkward situation. Others might advise you to settle the capital on your wife's relatives, so that if you were to die it would not go to your own family, and meanwhile to enjoy the usufruct during your own lifetime. But laws exist, and those laws do not grant you either the usufruct or the capital. My advice is: be an honest man and abide by the law. If it means the poorhouse for you, then so be it.

MYSELF

"Laws exist"! And such laws!

MY FATHER

What is your answer to the problem, Monsieur the Mathematician?

THE MATHEMATICIAN

My friend, did you not tell us that you had kept 20,000 francs for yourself?

THE HATTER

Yes, Sir.

THE MATHEMATICIAN

And roughly how much did your wife's illness cost you?

THE HATTER

About the same.

THE MATHEMATICIAN

Very well. Subtract 20,000 francs from 20,000 francs, and the remainder is zero.

MY FATHER (TO ME)

What does philosophy have to say?

MYSELF

Philosophy is silent when the law has no common sense.

My father sensed that he had better not press me, and, turning to the hatter, he said: "Master so-and-so, you admit that since you laid hands on your wife's estate you have lost all peace of mind: well then, what use is that money to you, if it robs you of the greatest gift of all? Get rid of it quickly and drink, eat, sleep, work, and be happy—at home, if that is possible, or elsewhere, if not."

The hatter replied brusquely: "No, Monsieur, I shall go away, I shall go to Geneva." — "And you expect to leave your remorse behind?" — "I don't know; but I shall go to Geneva." — "Go wherever you choose, conscience will infallibly follow you."

The hatter left, and his strange reply became the subject of debate. We agreed that perhaps distance in space or time weakened all feelings and all sorts of guilty conscience, even of crime. The assassin, removed to the shores of China, can no longer see the corpse which he left bleeding on the banks of the Seine. Remorse springs perhaps less from horror of oneself than from fear of others; less from shame at what one has done than from the blame and punishment it would bring if it were found out; and what criminal, however securely concealed, does not fear betrayal by some unexpected accident or careless word? How can he be sure he will not betray himself in delirium or fever or while asleep? Let someone hear him, near the scene of the crime, and he is undone; but those round him in China will not understand. "The days of a wicked man (said my father) are full of terrors. Calm of mind belongs only to the good man. He alone lives and dies in peace."

With this topic exhausted, the visitors left, my brother and sister returned, and we continued our interrupted conversation. My father said, "God be praised! Here we are together. I like to be with other people, but I like it still more to be with you." Then, to me: "Why did you not give the hatter your opinion?" — "Because you would not let me." — "Was I wrong not to?" — "No, because there is no advising a fool. Think of it! Is that man not his wife's closest relation? Had the property he kept not been brought to him as a dowry? Would it not have belonged to him by perfect legal right? What rights have those distant relatives?"

MY FATHER

You see only the outside of the law, not its deeper meaning.

MYSELF

I see what you see, Father; I see how insecure women would feel, how their husband would scorn and hate them, rightly or wrongly, if their death would rob him of their property. Suppose I am a decent man who has always done his best for his wife. Is not losing her enough in the way of unhappiness? Do I have to be robbed as well?

MY FATHER

But if you recognize the wisdom of the Law, you must obey it, so it seems to me.

MY SISTER

Without law, there would be no such thing as robbery.

MYSELF

Sister, you are wrong.

THE ABBÉ

Without the law, everything would belong to everybody and there would be no more property.

MYSELF

Brother, you are wrong.

THE ABBÉ

What is the basis of property, then?

MYSELF

By origin, it is taking possession of a thing by one's labor. Nature made good laws from the beginning of time. Force that ensures obedience to these laws is legitimate, and such force, all-powerful against the wicked man, must never be employed against the good man. I am that good man; and in these circumstances, and in many others I could mention, I summon that force before the bar of my own heart and reason and conscience and before the bar of natural equity. I question it, I submit to it, or I annul it.

MY FATHER

Preach those doctrines from the rooftops and, I promise you, you will make your fortune—and you will see their wonderful consequences!

MYSELF

I shall not preach them. There are truths which are not suited to fools. But I shall follow them as regards myself.

MY FATHER

As regards yourself, the man of wisdom!

MYSELF

Precisely.

MY FATHER

So I gather you would not approve too much of my conduct in the curé Thivet affair?

Abbé, what do you think of it?

THE ABBÉ

I think, Father, that it was prudent of you to consult Father Bouin and to listen to him; and that if you had followed your first instinct, you would undoubtedly have ruined us.

MY FATHER (TO ME)

Whereas you, great Philosopher, are not of that opinion?

MYSELF

No.

MY FATHER

That's rather brief. Tell me more.

MYSELF

You insist?

MY FATHER

I do.

MYSELF

I am to be perfectly frank?

MY FATHER

Most certainly.

MYSELF

Well then (I replied heatedly) I most certainly am not of that opinion. I think that if ever you did a bad action in your life, it was then; and that if, after destroying the will, you were going to feel obliged to recompense the legatee, you should have felt much more obliged to recompense the heirs, for *not* destroying it.

MY FATHER

I must admit that decision of mine has always weighed on my mind. But remember... Father Bouin!

MYSELF

Your Father Bouin, for all his reputation for learning and sanctity, was just a muddler, a narrow-minded bigot.

MY SISTER (IN A WHISPER)

Would you have liked to see us ruined?

MY FATHER

There, there; leave Father Bouin out of it. Tell us your arguments, without unkindness to any man.

MYSELF

My arguments? They are very simple. Here they are. Either the testator, as everything would seem to suggest, wanted to undo what he had done in the hardness of his heart, and you have spoiled his repentance; or he wanted it to take effect, and you abetted him in his injustice.

MY FATHER

His injustice! That is easily said.

MYSELF

Yes, yes, his injustice. For what Father Bouin said to you was mere empty subtleties, meager conjectures, "perhapses" of no substance or value, when one thinks of the actual circumstances, which so discredited the document you resurrected from the dust of ages. A box full of papers, and among them an ancient one invalidated by its date, by its injustice, by being mixed up with the other papers, by the death of the executors, by the indifference toward the legatee's letters, by the wealth of that legatee and the poverty of the rightful heirs.... What have we to weight against this? Some supposed restitution! So we are to imagine this poor devil of a priest, who did not have a farthing when he arrived in his parish and who spent eighty years of his life amassing, *sou* by *sou,* a hundred thousand francs, somehow managing to rob the Frémins, with whom he had never lived and whom he perhaps only knew by name, of such a sum? And say he really had done so, would that be so very...? I would have burnt that iniquitous document. Duty demanded that it be burnt. Duty required you to listen to your heart, which has been in pain ever since—a heart which knew better than that imbecile Buoin, whose advice proves the terrible sway of religious prejudice over even well-balanced minds, and the pernicious influence of unjust laws and fallacious principles on good sense and natural equity. If you had been sitting beside the curé when he was drawing up that iniquitous will, would you not have torn it up? Yet when fate places it in our hands, you preserve it.

MY FATHER

What if the curé had made you his residuary legatee?

MYSELF

I would have torn up the wretched document even sooner.

MY FATHER

I don't doubt it. But is there no difference between a bequest to you and a bequest to somebody else?

MYSELF

None. They are both either just or unjust, well-intentioned or ill-intentioned.

MY FATHER

If the law prescribes that, after a decease, every paper without exception must be listed and read, surely there must be some reason? What would you say the reason was?

MYSELF

If I wanted to be sarcastic I would say, to eat up the heirs' substance by consultation fees. But remember, you were not a lawyer, you were not bound by legal procedure: all that was expected of you was good will and natural equity.

My sister said nothing but squeezed my hand in token of approval. The abbé shook his ears, and my father said: "Another little insult to Father Bouin.

MY FATHER

Do you suppose my religion would approve of my conduct."

MYSELF

I do; and so much the worse for religion.

MY FATHER

Do you think that that document which you would burn on your own private authority would be declared valid in a court of law?

MYSELF

Possibly; and so much the worse for the law.

MY FATHER

You admit that the court might take no account of all the circumstances you make so much of?

MYSELF

I can't say; but I would at least have wanted them to be aired. I would have given fifty *louis* to have the will contested on behalf of those poor heirs. It would have been a good deed.

MY FATHER

Oh, as for that, if you had been there to advise it—though fifty *louis* is quite a sum for a man not long started in the world—the chances are I would have done it.

THE ABBÉ

As for me, I would have been as ready to give that money to the heirs themselves as to some lawyer.

MYSELF

You think we would have lost the case?

THE ABBÉ

I have no doubt of it. Judges, just like my father and Father Bouin, stick strictly to the law, and they do well. Judges, in such cases, shut their eyes to the particular circumstances, as my father and Father Bouin did, for fear of complications; and they do well. Sometimes, like my father and Father Bouin, and against their own conscience, they sacrifice the interests of the unfortunate and the innocent, since to do otherwise might encourage a hundred rascals; and they do well. They are afraid, as my father and Father Bouin were afraid, to pass a judgment which would be equitable in a given case and disastrous in a thousand others, opening the door to all sorts of disorders; and they do well. And in the case of this will...

MY FATHER (TO ME)

Your reasons, as coming from a private person, were perhaps good; but they would be bad coming from a public one. A not too scrupulous lawyer might have said to me, in private, "Burn that will"; but he would never have said so in writing.

MYSELF

I understand. It was an affair that ought never to have gone before the judges. And by God, it wouldn't have done, if I had been in your place!

MY FATHER

You would have preferred your own reason to public reason, the opinion of a Man as such to that of a man of law?

MYSELF

Of course. Were there not Men before there were men of law? Is not the reason of the human species a hundred times more sacred than the reason of some legislator? We call ourselves civilized, and we are worse than savages. It seems that for centuries we shall have to go lurching from one folly, one extravagance, to another, to arrive where the first spark of judgment, simple instinct, would have brought us direct. We are so thoroughly confused...

MY FATHER

My son, my son, reason is a good pillow, but, I find my head rests even better on the pillow of religion and the law. Not another word, please; I have no wish for a sleepless night.

But I have the impression you are riled. Tell me, if I had burnt the will, would you have stopped me making restitution?

MYSELF

No, Father; your peace of mind is rather more dear to me than all the property in the world.

MY FATHER

It pleases me to hear you say so, and for a particular reason.

MYSELF

Are you going to tell us what it is?

MY FATHER

Gladly. Your uncle Canon Vigneron[12] was a hard man, a very difficult man with his colleagues, always making malicious fun of them by words or deeds. It was planned that you should succeed to his prebend, by his making a demission in your favor, but in case the Chapter might thwart this, the family decided to send the document to Rome. A messenger set out, but your uncle died an hour or two before his arrival could be presumed. So there was a canonry and 1,800 francs a year lost. Your mother and aunts, all our friends and relatives indeed, said we ought to withhold the news of your uncle's death. I rejected their advice and had the church bells rung immediately.

MYSELF

And you did rightly.

MY FATHER

If I had listened to those good women and felt remorse later, I gather you would have sacrificed your canon's stall without hesitation, for the sake of my peace of mind.

MYSELF

I would have done it without that. Better to be a good philosopher—better to be nothing—than to be a bad canon.

The fat Prior returned and said, echoing my last words, "A bad canon! I wonder what it means to be a good or a bad prior, or a good or a bad canon? It is so hard to see the difference." My father shrugged his shoulders and left the room, to perform the rest of his day's devotions. The Prior remarked: "I'm afraid I have slightly shocked Papa."

THE ABBÉ

I think you may have done.

(Taking a book out of his pocket) I shall read you some pages from a description of Sicily by Father Labat.[13]

MYSELF

I know it. It's the story of the cobbler of Messina.

THE ABBÉ

Exactly.

THE PRIOR

What did this cobbler do?

THE ABBÉ

The story goes that, having been brought up virtuous and a friend to order and justice, he had much to endure in a country where the law was not merely weak but hardly existed at all. Every day was marked by some crime. Known assassins walked about with head high, braving the public's indignation. Parents were in despair over their daughters, seduced and reduced to the streets by cruel ravishers. Working men and their children were robbed of subsistence by monopolies. Every kind of extortion was in operation, wringing tears from the oppressed citizenry. The culprits escaped punishment through their connections or their money or through legal subterfuges. The shoemaker saw all that. It made his heart bleed, and all day at his bench he dreamed of how to put an end to it.

THE PRIOR

What could a poor devil like him do?

THE ABBÉ

You will find out. One day he set up a court of justice in his shop.

THE PRIOR

How did he do that?

MYSELF

The Prior thinks stories should get on, like himself reading Matins.

THE PRIOR

And why not? The art of oratory prescribes brevity, and the Gospel says, let thy prayer be brief.[14]

THE ABBÉ

When he heard of some atrocious crime, he found out the details and conducted a rigorous and secret investigation. Then, his double function of advocate and judge fulfilled, the trial concluded and the sentence passed, he would go out with a harquebus under his cloak and—by day, if he found them in their hideouts, or at night, if they were on their rounds—he would, with most admirable equity, let them have five or six balls through their carcasses.

THE PRIOR

I am afraid you are going to tell us this fine fellow ended his days broken on the wheel. I shall be sorry to hear that.

THE ABBÉ

After an execution he would leave the corpse where it was, without approaching closer and with the contentment of mind of someone who has shot a mad dog.

THE PRIOR

Did he kill many such mad dogs?

THE ABBÉ

He had killed more than fifty, and all highly placed, when the Viceroy offered a reward of 2,000 crowns to anyone who informed on him, and he swore before the altar to pardon the culprit if he gave himself up.

THE PRIOR

Which only a fool would do.

THE ABBÉ

Fearing that suspicion and punishment might fall on the innocent...

THE PRIOR

... he presented himself before the Viceroy?

THE ABBÉ

... and spoke to him as follows. "I have done your duty for you. I have had to be the one to condemn to death the criminals you should have punished. Here are the trial proceedings, setting forth their crimes. You will observe I have observed judicial procedure. I was tempted to begin with yourself but I was restrained by respect for the august master you represent. My life is in your hands, do with me what you will.

THE PRIOR

And what did he do with him?

THE ABBÉ

I don't know. All I know is, that with all his marvelous zeal for justice, that man was no more than a murderer.

THE PRIOR

A murderer! That is a harsh name. What other word would be left to describe him if he had assassinated decent people?

MYSELF

Lunacy!

MY SISTER

One could wish...

THE ABBÉ (TO ME)

Imagine you are king and the case is submitted to you for your judgment. What is your decision?

MYSELF

Abbé, you are laying a trap for me, and I shall fall into it cheerfully. I condemn the Viceroy to become the cobbler and the cobbler to become the Viceroy.

MY SISTER

Very good, dear brother.

My father reappeared with that serene look he always wears after his prayers. We told him the story, and he supported the abbé's verdict. My sister commented: "So Messina loses, if not her only just man, at least her only gallant citizen. I find that sad."

Supper was served. They went on arguing against me for a while. We teased the Prior a good deal about his decision in the hatter's case and his low opinion of priors and canons. We put the question of the will to him, and instead of offering any solution, he told us a story of his own.

THE PRIOR

You remember that great bankruptcy of Bourmont's, the money-lender?

MY FATHER

Remember it? I was one of the creditors.

THE PRIOR

So much the better.

MY FATHER

Why so?

THE PRIOR

Because if I did wrong, it will help to soothe my conscience. I was appointed chief creditor. Among Bourmont's assets was a bill for 100 crowns in the name of one of his neighbors, a grain merchant. This bill, had the proceeds been shared pro rata among the many creditors, would have brought them about twelve *sous* apiece, whereas it would have spelled ruin for the merchant. I told myself...

MY FATHER

... that none of the creditors would have grudged the unlucky fellow twelve *sous*, so you tore the bill up and gave him alms stolen from my pocket?

THE PRIOR

Yes, I did. Are you angry with me?

MY FATHER

No.

THE PRIOR

Have the goodness to believe that the rest would have been no more angry than you, and then all is said.

MY FATHER

But, Monsieur the Prior, if you tear up one bill on your own private authority, why not tear up two, three, four, as many as there are poor folk to help at others' expense? That principle of pity could lead us a long way, Monsieur the Prior. Justice, justice...

THE PRIOR

... is often a great injustice.

A young woman who lived on the floor above came down. She was gaiety and folly in person. My father asked her for news of her husband. This husband was a libertine, who had given his wife a bad example which she had, I think, to some extent followed, and he had gone to Martinique to escape his creditors. Madame d'Isigny (for that was our lodger's name) replied: "Monsieur d'Isigny? God be praised, I haven't heard a word of him. Perhaps he got drowned."

THE PRIOR

Drowned. I congratulate you.

MADAME D'ISIGNY

Why should it matter to you, Monsieur Prior?

THE PRIOR

For no reason. But how about you?

MADAME D'ISIGNY

How do you mean, me?

THE PRIOR

People say...

MADAME D'ISIGNY

What do they say?

THE PRIOR

Since you insist: they say that he found certain letters of yours....

MADAME D'ISIGNY

And do I not have a fine collection of his?

Whereupon there was a comical quarrel between the Prior and Madame d'Isigny on the privileges of the two sexes. Madame d'Isigny called on me for support, and I undertook to prove to the Prior that the first of two spouses to break their vows gave carte blanche to the other. But my father called for his nightcap, broke up the conversation, and sent us all to bed. When it was my turn to bid him goodnight, I whispered as I kissed him: "Father, the truth is, there are no laws for the wise man." — "Not so loud," said my father. — "All laws being subject to exceptions, it is for the wise man to judge when they should be obeyed and when they should be broken."

MY FATHER

I should not be too sorry if there were one or two in the town like you; but I should not want to live there if they all thought the same.

NOTES

Introduction

1. Honoré de Balzac, in the *Revue Parisienne,* quoted by M. L. Charles in "The Growth of Diderot's Fame in France from 1784 to 1875" (Ph.D. diss., Bryn Mawr, 1942), 76–77.

2. Johann Wolfgang van Goethe, *Autobiography,* trans. John Oxenford (Chicago: University of Chicago Press, 1974), 2:106.

3. Ibid.

4. Letter from J.-B. Suard to the Margrave of Bayreuth, March 30, 1773; quoted by G. Roth in his edition of Diderot's *Correspondance,* 16 vols. (Paris: Editions de Minuit, 1955–1970), 12:202.

5. In Ian Watt's *The Rise of the Novel: Studies in Defoe, Richardson, and Fielding* (Berkeley: University of California Press, 1957) and Michael McKeon's *The Origins of the English Novel, 1600–1740* (Baltimore: Johns Hopkins University Press, 1987).

6. Pierre-Honore Robbé de Beauveset (1712–1792), a scurrilous satirical poet.

7. Michel Butor, "Diderot le fataliste et ses maitres," in *Repertoire* (Paris: Editions de Minuit, 1968), 3.

8. Louis-Antoine de Bougainville, *Voyage autour du monde,* ed. Jacques Proust (Paris: Gallimard, 1982), 230.

9. Claude Lévi-Strauss, *Tristes tropiques* (Paris: Plon, 1955), 351.

This Is Not a Story

Included, in part, in the manuscript periodical *La Correspondance littéraire* in April 1773. First appeared in printed form in Diderot, *Oeuvres,* ed. Jacques-André Naigeon (1798).

1. *Sovereign Council of the Cape.* This body included the governor-general of Santo Domingo, the intendant, and various military and legal officials.

2. *Maurepas.* Jean-Frederic Phélypeaux, Comte de Maurepas; he held, among other high posts, the secretaryship of state for the navy, 1725–1749. A French commercial establishment in St. Petersburg was in fact under consideration in 1747.

3. *d'Hérouville.* Antoine de Ricouart, Comte d'Hérouville (1713–1782) published under his own name a *Treatise on Legions, on the Model of the Ancient Romans* in 1757. Earlier editions had appeared under the name of the Maréchal de Saxe. His wife "Lolotte," Louise Gaucher (c. 1725–1765), had been an actress and singer and had had a number of illegitimate children by Lord Albemarle. "Society" never accepted her, and she died disconsolate.

4. *Montucla.* Jean Etienne de Montucla (1725–1799) published a *History*

of Research into Squaring the Circle in 1754, and in 1758 a *History of Mathematics.*

5. *Gardeil.* Jean-Baptiste Gardeil (d. 1808) was a real person. After a penurious youth he became professor of medicine and member of the Academy of Sciences at Toulouse. He spent thirty years on a translation of Hippocrates.

6. *Mademoiselle de la Chaux.* She, too, was a real person, a friend of the mathematician Jean le Rond d'Alembert, with whom Diderot collaborated on the *Encyclopédie,* and the philosopher Etienne de Condillac, another friend of Diderot's. Two or three months after Diderot published his *Letter on the Deaf and Dumb* in February 1751, he printed some *Additions in Clarification of Certain Portions of the "Letter on the Deaf and Dumb,"* containing a long and brilliant letter addressed to Mlle de la Chaux, answering some objections raised by her.

7. *Deschamps.* Anne-Marie Pagès, known as La Deschamps, was a dancer at the Opera and had a whole succession of rich lovers, among them a brother-in-law of Diderot's mistress Sophie Volland. She was wildly extravagant and in 1760 had to sell her *hôtel* and her furniture to pay her debts.

8. *Le Camus.* Antoine de Camus (1722–1772) was a scholar and man of letters as well as a physician. Diderot, in his *Elements of Physiology,* mentions Camus' overenthusiasm for bleeding and other drastic treatments.

9. *Hume.* Mlle de la Chaux translated several of Hume's *Philosophical Essays,* under the title *Essais sur le commerce, le luxe, l'argent* (Amsterdam, 1752).

10. *Pompadour.* The Marquise de Pompadour died in 1764, aged forty-three. Diderot had had some slight acquaintance with her.

On the Inconsistency of Public Opinion

1. *Grand' Chambre.* The *Grand' Chambre* was the earliest founded of the chambers of *Parlement. La Tournelle,* essentially a criminal court, was one of the chambers of *Parlement* through which members passed in turn.

2. *the tyrant's own adopted son.* The Roman emperor Galba had adopted Piso Licinianus in preference to Otho and had made him Caesar. Galba was then assassinated, and Piso, who took refuge in the Temple of Vesta, was seized and assassinated also, while the crowd paid homage to Otho. Piso had reigned for five days.

Supplement to Bougainville's *Voyage*

Included in *Correspondance littéraire,* September–October 1773 and March–April 1774. First published in printed form, with derogatory remarks about Diderot's sansculotte tendencies, in the *Opuscules philosophiques* of Bourlet de Vauxcelles in 1796.

1. *At quanto . . . .* "But how much better—how utterly contrary to this—is the course that Nature, rich in her own resources, suggests, if you want to behave properly and not confuse what should be desired with what should be

avoided! Do you think it does not matter whether the fault lies with you or with circumstances?"

2. *a brazen monster.* It is not quite clear which of several incidents in Bougainville's *Voyage* is referred to here.

3. *birds come and perch.* Bougainville mentions the lack of fear of humans shown by wild geese on the Falkland Islands.

4. *once joined up.* Buffon had put forward similar theories in his *Theory of the Earth* (1749).

5. *"The Lancers."* A little island in the Pomotou archipelago, discovered by Bougainville and so named because the inhabitants brandished long pikes.

6. *crushed, under the feet of a priestess.* Montesquieu, in his *Spirit of Laws,* book 23, chapter 16, describes this as a birth-control custom in Formosa.

7. *Jesuits.* One of the most vivid chapters in Bougainville's *Voyage* describes the extraordinary colonial empire established by Jesuit missionaries in Paraguay and Uruguay. He is torn between admiration for the moral dominance achieved by the Jesuits without force of arms and horror at the servility and mental passivity to which they had reduced the Indians. As Diderot's text suggests, Bougainville arrived just at the time that, as a consequence of a general boycotting of the Jesuits in Europe, the king of Spain was taking forcible steps to abolish their regime in South America.

8. *Patagonians.* The legend that Patagonians were giants goes back to Magellan. Matthew Maty, secretary to the Royal Society, had recently published a *Letter* to the explorer and mathematician Charles-Marie de la Condamine on the subject. When Bougainville went on shore with a landing party in Tierra del Fuego, six Patagonians rushed up crying "chaoua." "On joining us they pressed their outstretched palms against ours and hugged us. . . . These good folk seemed overjoyed at our arrival" (*Voyage,* part 1, chapter 8).

9. *Aotourou.* Bougainville took Aotourou to Paris, where he lived for a year (March 1769–March 1770), was presented to Louis XV, and acquired a taste for the opera, which he would attend on his own and dressed in European clothes. Bougainville made generous provision for his return to Tahiti, but he died of smallpox on the homeward journey.

10. *all things belong to all men.* Bougainville's officers were all inclined to believe they had found primitive communism in Tahiti.

11. *This country belongs to us.* Bougainville relates how he had an act of possession of the island inscribed on an oaken tablet, which was buried near the shore (part 2, chapter 3.)

12. *infected our blood.* There was much acrimonious debate as to who brought venereal disease to the island. Bougainville, as against Diderot's *Supplement,* asserts that it was rife there when he arrived and that the Tahitians infected his crew with it.

13. *a woman disguised as a man.* Jeanne Baret had joined the crew of the *Etoile* as the servant of the naturalist Philibert Commerson.

14. *Chaplain.* Bougainville himself gives no information about the Chaplain, except that he was named La Vèze.

15. *religion.* According to Bougainville the Tahitians in fact recognized a sun-god and a moon-god and venerated idols.

16. *Polly Baker.* The story of Polly Baker was a fabrication by Benjamin Franklin, in an article in the *London Magazine* in April 1747. It was cited as a true story in the *History of the Two Indies* (1770) by Diderot's friend the abbé Raynal, a work in the later editions of which Diderot would have a considerable hand.

17. *black veils.* In Bougainville's account the black veils merely indicated mourning.

18. *Venice.* Diderot no doubt got his adverse opinion of the Venetian government from Raynal's *History of the Two Indies.*

19. *Mercury's lyre.* The Greek lyre player Terpander was fined by the ephors and his lyre nailed to the wall because he had dared to add another string to the instrument.

The Two Friends from Bourbonne

1. *Hastenbeck.* The French victory at Hastenbeck (July 26, 1757) was one of the most famous battles of the Seven Year's War.

2. *smuggling.* Bourbonne was on the frontiers of Champagne, Lorraine, and Franche-Comté and so a favorite spot for smugglers. Champagne was one of the five "great farms" of the kingdom which traded freely with one another; Alsace, Lorraine, and Franche-Comté, being recent additions to France, traded freely abroad but were separated from the rest of France by a customs barrier. Smugglers, such as the famous leader of brigands Louis Mandrin (1724–1755), tended to become popular heroes.

3. *tribunals.* At the request of the farmers-general, a special jurisdiction for smuggling offenses was set up in 1733, first for cases of armed smuggling and later for fiscal and financial crimes generally. Its procedure was secret, and defendants did not have the right of legal representation; its decisions were speedy and without appeal. Other similar jurisdictions soon followed. The one at Rheims was active 1740–1788.

4. *Coleau.* Coleau (or Colleau) was *lieutenant-criminel* at the *châtelet* of Melun. He held his powers directly from the King's Council. The installation of Coleau and his commission, none of whom belonged to the Champagne area, aroused hostility not only among the "people" but among the local legal establishment, who were jealous of the encroachment on their prerogatives.

5. *maréchaussée.* The *maréchaussée* was a mounted police force. It was quite distinct from the other adversary of the smugglers, the vast body of armed men employed by the farmers-general.

6. *Iroquois.* An allusion to Saint-Lambert's "The Two Friends: a Tale of the Iroquois" (see Introduction, p. 3).

7. *Testalunga.* The story of Testalunga and Romano is related by J. H. de Riedesel in his *Reise durch Sicilien und Gross-Griechenland* (1771), a book which gave rise to a Romantic interest in Sicily, as home of the "natural man."

8. *Aubert.* The subdelegate Aubert (a *subdélégué* was a subordinate to the intendant) was a real person.

9. *rushed from one spot to another.* Herbert Dieckmann suggests that Schiller was remembering this passage when writing act 2 of *The Robbers.*

10. *Fourmont.* He really existed and was a *conseiller* at the *Présidial* at Chaumont. Diderot intervened in a complicated legal quarrel between him and the famous *salonnière* Mme Geoffrin; he was rude about Fourmont in letters to Sophie Volland, calling him an "arrant boor" and other names.

11. *Vergier.* Jacques Vergier (1655–1720), author of frivolous *contes.*

12. *Hamilton.* R. Anthony Hamilton (1646–1720), born in Ireland of Scottish descent, took up residence in France in 1688. He wrote tales in the *Arabian Nights* style.

13. *Cailleau.* Diderot greatly admired the actor Joseph Cailleau (or Caillot) (1732–1816), regarding him as a supreme "imitator of nature" and mentioning him in his *Paradox of the Actor.*

14. *Treatise on the Human Mind.* Claude Adrien Helvetius's freethinking *De l'Esprit* was first published in 1759. Diderot, who was writing in 1770, presumably knew that a second edition was to appear shortly.

Conversation of a Father with His Children

1. *My father.* Diderot's father, Didier Diderot (1685–1759), was a master cutler in the town of Langres in Champagne. His surgical instruments enjoyed a national reputation. The "Abbé" of the "Conversation" represents Diderot's younger brother Didier-Pierre, who became an archdeacon. The term *abbé* is often used simply to mean "clergyman."

2. *my sister.* Denise Diderot (1715–1797), known in the family as "Soeurette." Diderot, whom she idolized, describes her as "lively, striving, gay, downright." She never left Langres and never married.

3. *Thivet.* The curé Antoine Charles was a real person, who died in 1733, having served the parish of Thivet since 1687.

4. *Frémins.* Diderot's fictional name for the Després, who had been printers and booksellers since the mid-seventeenth century.

5. *Cartouche or Nivet.* Louis-Dominque Bourguignon, known as Cartouche (1693–1721), was leader of a famous band of robbers and was finally broken on the wheel, as was the murderer Nivet.

6. *other brute beasts.* The passage, very freely rendered here, is in the work translated as *De sanitate tuenda.*

7. *plague at Marseilles.* The terrible epidemic of 1720–1721.

8. *Hadrian the Sixth.* The story of Pope Hadrian VI (1459–1523) and his unpopularity can be read in Ludwig von Pastor's *History of the Popes.* His doctor was named Antracino.

9. *Guénaut.* Francois Guénaut (1586–1667) was physician to Louis XII and Louis XIV as well as to Cardinal Mazarin.

10. *Verville's Merry Tales . . . Theological Monthly.* I am freely paraphrasing

Diderot, who refers to the *Moyen de parvenir,* a collection of rather broad tales by F. B. de Verville (1558–1612) and the *Conférences de Grenoble,* no doubt the proceedings of some theological colloquia.

11. *Dubois.* Louis Dubois was a friend of the Diderot family. Diderot consulted him on a legal point during a trip to Langres in 1754.

12. *Canon Vigneron.* Diderot's maternal uncle Didier Vigneron, one of the canons of the cathedral of Langres, died in 1728 when Diderot was fourteen.

13. *Labat.* The story is indeed in *Voyages du père Labat en Espagne et en Italie* (Paris, 1730), 5:188ff.

14. *let thy prayer be brief.* Cf. Matthew 6:6–7.